Mail Order Mediocrity

Book 60 in Brides of Beckham

Kirsten Osbourne

---

1. http://www.kirstenandmorganna.com

Chapter One

The afternoon sun bathed the room in a warm, golden light as Deborah's nimble fingers danced over her latest knitting project. Surrounded by the soft clicking of needles and the hum of friendly chatter, the parlor of Mrs. Agatha Jackson's orphanage was a cozy haven for the ten young women who called it home.

"Deborah, that's lovely," Amy remarked, peering over her shoulder with a tray of freshly baked cookies in hand. The scent of cinnamon and sugar filled the air, mingling with the laughter and conversation of their make-shift family.

"Thank you," Deborah murmured, her cheeks tinged with modesty. She rarely looked up from her work, but the pride in her eyes was unmistakable.

"Can't wait to wear it," Brenda chimed in, green eyes sparkling with mischief as she teased Deborah gently.

"Behave, Brenda," Erna scolded lightly, though her eyes crinkled with mirth.

"Surely will, ma'am," Brenda replied with an exaggerated tip of an imaginary hat, eliciting giggles from around the room.

"Imagine all of us living near one another, married with men of our own. No kids for me, of course, but marriage sounds lovely," Cassandra sighed, her voice tinged with longing as she helped Gail untangle a skein of yarn.

"And we'd all have servants, instead of being servants," Faith added, smoothing out a wrinkle in the tablecloth.

"I love that idea," Hannah agreed, smiling at Mrs. Jackson, the silver-haired woman who presided over the orphanage with a grace that made each girl feel cherished.

"Why did I spend all this time learning to bake bread and darn socks if I'm going to have servants anyway?" Imogene asked.

"Because those are skills every lady should have," Amy said, placing the cookies on the table. "Helps in life and love."

Jane, the youngest, watched the exchange with wide-eyed wonder, her own knitting forgotten in her lap. She'd just finished school, and was happy to say that Cassandra was no longer her teacher.

"Come now, everyone, let's enjoy these treats Amy's prepared," Mrs. Jackson said, guiding them together like a mother hen with her brood.

As they gathered, the distance between Deborah and the rest of the world seemed to lessen, her shyness melting away in the nurturing environment that Mrs. Jackson fostered. Here, among her sisters, she found a place where her quiet spirit was not just accepted, but celebrated. And perhaps, in time, the outside world would learn to appreciate her too.

DAWN'S FIRST LIGHT spilled through the gauzy curtains of the orphanage, casting a soft glow on the faces of sleeping children. All thirty children who called the foundling home their own woke to the familiar routine that bound them together. They dressed in simple garb, whispering and giggling, their camaraderie woven into each shared chore and whispered secret.

Deborah slipped quietly between the beds, her slender fingers deftly folding blankets into crisp rectangles. Her gaze lingered for a moment on the sleeping forms of her closest friends—Amy, Cassandra, Brenda, Erna, Faith, Gail, Hannah, Imogene, and young Jane—before she gathered her shawl and stepped into the cool morning air.

The walk to the general store was a silent affair. Deborah's thoughts were varied and active as always, just like the winding path that led her into town. At the store, she tucked herself behind the counter, her hands busy with stocking shelves and tidying goods. Her boss, Mr. Welling, often furrowed his brow at her hesitance to engage with customers, particularly the male patrons who seemed to turn her voice to a whisper.

"Deborah, you've got to speak up," he'd say, not unkindly. "Folks won't bite, you know."

She would nod, a faint blush coloring her cheeks, and continue her work with quiet efficiency. She'd worked at the store for two years, and she still couldn't get used to talking to men. She'd rarely been around men, mostly just boys at school and at the foundling home. She hoped that someday she wouldn't be so afraid to voice her thoughts, but that day seemed very far off.

BACK AT THE ORPHANAGE, the buzz of excitement was palpable as Mrs. Jackson summoned Deborah to her office, a rare event that could only mean something extraordinary. Deborah entered, her heart fluttering, to find Mrs. Jackson beaming from behind her desk.

"Deborah," Mrs. Jackson began, her eyes twinkling. "I need your help. We're hosting a dance in Texas, a grand event to bring people together. I believe it might be a wonderful opportunity for you."

"Me?" Deborah's voice was barely audible, her fingers twisting the hem of her apron. "I don't go to dances."

"Yes, you! It's high time the world saw the wonderful young woman you've become. And who knows," she added with a wink, "perhaps love is waiting for you under those Texas stars."

Deborah's mind whirled with the possibilities, her previous night's dreams intertwining with this unexpected chance. The thought of dancing, of laughter and music, sent a thrill through her that was both exhilarating and terrifying.

"Think it over," Mrs. Jackson encouraged. "There's no rush."

As word of the dance spread through the orphanage, the girls buzzed with questions and daydreams about suitors and gowns. Even Deborah found herself caught in the tide of enthusiasm, her reservations ebbing as she imagined the warmth of the Texas summer, the sound of fiddles, and perhaps, just perhaps, the touch of a hand leading her onto the dance floor.

Oh, how she hoped she would be able to follow a man to the floor and allow him to touch her without throwing up on his feet. Embarrassing herself that way would be truly tragic.

DEBORAH TWIRLED THE yarn between her fingers, the soft click-clack of knitting needles a comforting cadence against the hum of conversation. The other girls were excited, their excitement palpable in the sunlit parlor of the orphanage. But beneath Deborah's calm exterior lay a roiling sea of trepidation.

"Imagine all those cowboys," Amy gushed, "tall and handsome!" Deborah knew that Amy wanted a family of her own more than anything. Amy was calm and difficult to ruffle, and Deborah could see her with her own children. It was easy to imagine.

"Yes," Deborah murmured, eyes on her knitting, imagining instead the vast, open Texas skies that awaited them.

"Deb, you'll be the belle of the ball with your dainty stitches!" Cassandra grinned, leaning over to admire the delicate patterns emerging from Deborah's nimble work.

"Hardly," Deborah replied softly, a faint blush coloring her cheeks. "It's just knitting."

"More than 'just,' I'd say," Brenda chimed in, casting a knowing glance Deborah's way.

A hush fell as they turned to see Mrs. Jackson enter, her presence always commanding gentle respect.

"Girls, remember, this dance is about new beginnings," Mrs. Jackson reminded them. "It's a chance to find family, love—"

"Or both!" Erna interjected, earning a chorus of giggles.

But for Deborah, the mention of love knotted her stomach tight. Her past experiences had been frayed at best. She'd been adopted for a year before she was returned. She remembered a father who was a whisper of a memory, who had run off when she'd been little and a mother's suitor whose eyes had lingered too long, his hands too eager. She shied away from those memories, focusing on the steady rhythm of knit and purl.

"Jane, my dear," Mrs. Jackson said softly, turning to the youngest of the group, "you know you're not to join the others in Texas."

Jane nodded, her expression tinged with disappointment. "I understand, Mrs. Jackson. Eighteen feels so far away."

"Your time will come," Mrs. Jackson assured her, placing an affectionate hand on Jane's shoulder.

"Will it?" Deborah thought, her heart aflutter with unease. "Can time unravel the past?"

"Deborah, are you all right?" Hannah asked, noticing her friend's distant gaze.

"Of course," Deborah answered, her voice a whisper lost in the chatter of hopeful hearts.

"Texas will be grand," Faith added, trying to coax a smile from Deborah. "New people, new places..."

"New fears," Deborah nearly said aloud but caught herself.

"Perhaps," she conceded instead, her smile more a promise to herself than a reflection of joy. She decided then. She would go to Texas, not for romance, but for the hope that maybe, just maybe, the dance could help her learn to face her fears.

DEBORAH STOOD BEFORE the cracked mirror, tugging at the hem of her simple cotton dress. The fabric felt rough against her fingertips, a stark contrast to the delicate yarns she was accustomed to weaving into warmth. Her reflection showed a woman, barely past girlhood, with tendrils of brown hair escaping the practical bun at the nape of her neck.

"Looks fine to me," Amy commented from behind her, her voice brimming with the same enthusiasm that filled the room.

"Thank you, Amy," Deborah replied, her words careful and measured.

"Are you excited?" Cassandra asked, bustling about with last-minute preparations.

"Excited... yes, and nervous," Deborah confessed, allowing herself a moment of honesty.

"Those men won't know what hit them!" Brenda chimed in, her laughter echoing around the walls of the dormitory they shared. Brenda had worked in Beckham as a nanny, but with the matchmaking dance coming up, she was back living in the foundling home with the others.

"Men are just people, like us," Gail said, catching Deborah's eye. Her tone was matter-of-fact, an attempt to bridge the gap between fear and reality. Only Cassandra knew that Deborah was afraid of men, but the others all knew she was shy around them. They often tried to help her feel better in social situations.

"Perhaps," Deborah murmured, her gaze drifting towards the window.

"Remember, it's just a dance," Hannah reminded her, her voice soothing like a lullaby.

"Right, just a dance," Deborah echoed.

"Promise us you'll try to have fun?" Faith pleaded, her eyes wide with concern for her friend.

"I promise," Deborah said, the words forming a pact she intended to keep. For her friends, for Mrs. Jackson, but most importantly, for herself.

"Good," Imogene added, her voice soft yet firm. "Because we're all rooting for you."

"Even Jane," Deborah thought, her chest tightening at the mention of the youngest among them, left behind due to the cruel constraint of time.

"Thank you, everyone," Deborah said, her gratitude interwoven with determination. She turned back to her reflection, seeing not just a shy orphan but a courageous soul ready to face the unknown.

"Let's show Texas what we're made of," she declared, more to herself than to anyone else.

Chapter Two

The ten sisters formed a semi-circle around the hearth. Jane, the youngest, fidgeted at the end of the line, her fingers nervously twisting the fabric of her dress. The heavy summer air seemed to buzz with expectation, the kind that precedes a long-awaited storm or, in their case, the arrival of Elizabeth Tandy.

"Will she be stern, do you think?" Jane's voice quivered slightly.

"Elizabeth Tandy? No, I've met her," Amy said with a reassuring smile. "She's sweeter than one of my pies."

As if on cue, the door swung open, and in breezed Elizabeth Tandy, with her striking blond hair and bright green eyes that instantly scanned the room, settling on each sister like a comforting touch. She wore a dress that managed to be both stylish and modest—a perfect mirror of her reputation as a professional yet nurturing matchmaker.

"Good afternoon, ladies!" Her voice was clear and confident, yet carried an undercurrent of genuine warmth. "I hope this day finds you well."

"Good afternoon, Mrs. Tandy," chorused the sisters, some with voices bold, others barely above a murmur.

"Please, call me Elizabeth. We're to be friends, after all," she said with a gentle chuckle, moving closer to the group.

She began engaging each sister in turn, leaning in with an attentiveness that made it seem as though, for that moment, they were the only two people in the world. To the more reticent among them, she used a softer tone, while with the bolder spirits, she matched their enthusiasm.

"And what do you seek in a husband, my dear?" Elizabeth asked one of the sisters, her gaze encouraging.

"Someone kind, someone who respects my mind as much as my cooking, I suppose," Cassandra said.

"Ah, a partnership of equals. Admirable!" Elizabeth nodded approvingly before turning to the next sister. "And you? What would bring you joy in marriage?"

"Adventure," Gail declared with a twinkle in her eye. "Life is too short for boredom."

"Yes, it is," agreed Elizabeth.

When Elizabeth reached Jane, the girl's heart fluttered like a trapped bird. "Mrs. T—Elizabeth, I mean, I don't quite know what to look for..."

"Jane, isn't it?" Elizabeth said softly, her intuition guiding her. "That's all right. Sometimes, it's not about looking, but being open to what comes your way."

"That sounds smart," Jane said.

"Exactly. And sometimes," Elizabeth continued, "the best matches are those we never could have dreamed up ourselves."

Deborah sat on the outskirts of the gathering, her fingers moving nimbly over the knitting needles. The soft clacking sound was a soothing counterpoint to the thrum of excited voices filling the room. She glanced up now and then, watching Elizabeth Tandy's easy smiles and listening to the laughter she drew from each of Deborah's sisters. Deborah's own smile was small, tentative – it was easier to retreat into the familiar patterns of yarn than risk the uncertainty of conversation.

"Deborah, isn't it?" The voice, warm and clear as a bell, pulled her gaze up. Elizabeth stood before her, a basket of colorful yarn resting on one hip. Deborah's heart skipped, but she managed a nod, her hands not missing a beat in their work.

"I see you're quite the knitter," Elizabeth observed, her eyes appreciative as they took in the intricate pattern emerging from the needles. "I have a feeling you put a lot of care into everything you do."

Deborah felt a blush rise to her cheeks. "It's just knitting," she murmured, her voice barely above a whisper.

"Ah, but it's more than that. It's an art," Elizabeth countered gently, pulling a chair close to sit down. "And if I may say so, I believe finding the right match for someone is a bit like knitting – it's about creating something beautiful from two very different strands."

Deborah laughed softly, the tension in her easing just a bit at the analogy. "I suppose that makes sense," she said.

"Deborah," Elizabeth said, leaning forward with sincerity lighting up her green eyes, "I understand that this whole process can seem frightening. But I promise you, we'll find someone who will value you for who you are, fears and all."

"Even if I'm... afraid of men?" Deborah asked softly.

"Especially then." Elizabeth's assurance was firm, kind. "Someone patient and gentle, who will give you the space to grow comfortable, at your own pace."

Deborah blinked rapidly, the kindness in Elizabeth's words weaving through her defenses. For the first time, she allowed herself to entertain the thought that maybe, just maybe, there could be a man out there who would understand her quiet ways.

"Thank you," Deborah finally said, her voice steadier than she felt. "I'll try to remember that."

Elizabeth patted her hand, a touch as light as a summer breeze. "That's all I ask." Rising from her seat, she added with a playful glint, "Now, don't let me keep you from your masterpiece. I expect to see a lovely pair of socks when you're done!"

With a soft chuckle, Deborah watched Elizabeth move away, her presence leaving a warmth that lingered in the air.

"Mrs. Tandy?" Deborah's voice was barely above a whisper, but it carried enough to halt Elizabeth in her tracks.

Elizabeth pivoted back, her green eyes locking onto Deborah with an attentive gaze. "Yes?"

"Suppose... suppose no one finds me agreeable?" Deborah's question hung between them, laden with the weight of her insecurities. "I'm just... I'm ordinary. And I'm skilled at naught but knitting."

"Deborah Brown," Elizabeth said, taking a step closer, her tone imbued with conviction. "You are far from ordinary. I look at you and I can almost feel your kindness wash over me. That's anything but ordinary."

"But I fear men won't see past..." Deborah trailed off, unable to articulate the shadow that lurked in her past.

"Love isn't about seeing past," Elizabeth replied gently. "It's about seeing within. The right man will cherish the very things that make you 'you.'"

"Thank you," Deborah murmured, feeling a curious lightness, as if the weight of doubt had lessened ever so slightly.

"Trust in the journey, Deborah," Elizabeth encouraged before turning her attention to the rest of the room, where the other sisters awaited her guidance.

"Hannah, what joy brings you to a man's company?" Elizabeth asked, her manner engaging and kind. Hannah, with her boisterous laughter, spoke of a love for dancing and lively evenings.

"Cassandra, what dreams do you whisper to the night sky?" Cassandra shared her longing for a partner who would allow her to start her own business, someone who wouldn't feel threatened by her need to be independent.

"Brenda, tell me, what strength do you seek in another?" Brenda's eyes twinkled as she confessed her desire for a man who could match her stubbornness with patience.

Deborah watched, listening to the hopes and aspirations unfolding around her. Elizabeth's talent for reading hearts, for weaving connections where none were seen, filled the room with the promise of what tomorrow might bring.

The ten sisters circled around Elizabeth Tandy, and Deborah could feel her sisters' excitement. Deborah stood slightly apart, her hands clasped together.

"Remember, girls," Elizabeth was saying, her voice a warm embrace, "the heart knows no distance. Texas may be far, but love will bridge any expanse."

"Does love also temper the heat?" Cassandra asked, fanning herself with a hand as if feeling the Texas sun already.

"Only the heat of loneliness, dear," chuckled Elizabeth, her green eyes dancing.

Jane's gaze fixed on Elizabeth. "We won't forget you," she promised, the youngest's resolve mirrored in her steady tone.

"Nor I you," replied Elizabeth, her smile soft yet confident. "Each of you is bound for a grand adventure. And don't forget, I'll be with you every step of the way. And Mrs. Jackson has decided to go as well!"

"Adventure?" asked Hannah, eyebrows arched. "I thought it was a dance."

"Life's greatest adventures often begin with a single step," Elizabeth countered sagely, her laughter mingling with theirs.

"Or a misstep," added Faith, ever the mirthful one, twirling in place. "Especially in my case."

"Then we'll just pick each other up," Amy said.

"Indeed," agreed Elizabeth, nodding. "You have each other, and that's more than most can boast."

"Will there be cowboys?" Imogene asked.

"Plenty," Elizabeth assured her, bending down to meet the girl's gaze. "But remember, a cowboy's charm is not just in his hat."

"Is it in his boots, then?" teased Deborah, surprising herself with a small grin.

"Perhaps," Elizabeth laughed, straightening. "But always look beyond the boots and hats to the heart beneath."

"Enough about hats and hearts," Amy said, with a practicality that matched her no-nonsense bun. "We have a train to catch."

"Right you are," Elizabeth said, stepping back as the sisters gathered their few belongings.

"Thank you, Elizabeth. For everything," Jane said, her voice carrying all their gratitude. "I don't like it that I can't join my sisters in Texas right away, but I'm so thankful you've made arrangements for me to

"Off you go, then," Elizabeth waved them toward the door, her blond hair catching the light like a halo.

"Texas awaits!" cheered Erna, leading the procession with a skip in her step.

"Goodbye, Elizabeth," they chorused as the older woman took her leave.

"Goodbye, my dears. I'll see you at the train station tomorrow," Elizabeth called as she walked out to her buggy.

The train ride seemed to take forever, but was also over much too soon in Deborah's eyes. Soon, they were getting ready for the dance, having taken over Susan Dailey's residence. Susan was Elizabeth's sister, and she had done a great deal to help organize the dance, making sure all the single men in the area knew what was happening.

Deborah put on the dress that had been provided, and though it felt strange to be dressed up as she was, she was more nervous about what she would do if asked to dance.

The air inside Susan Dailey's house crackled with anticipation, a flurry of activity as the women bustled about, making final adjustments to their dresses and smoothing down any stray hairs. The room was filled with the soft rustle of fabric and the gentle clink of jewelry as each sister added finishing touches to their attire. Deborah felt a bead of sweat trickle down her back, the heat of the Texas summer threatening to overwhelm her.

As the sisters prepared to walk to the church for the dance, Deborah couldn't shake off her apprehension. The thought of fainting from the oppressive heat loomed over her like a dark cloud, casting a shadow on the excitement of the evening. She glanced at Cassandra, who was adjusting a stray ribbon on her dress with practiced ease.

"Cassandra," Deborah began hesitantly, drawing her sister's attention. "Do you ever wonder about the men we might meet tonight?"

Cassandra turned to face Deborah, her expression contemplative. "I suppose I have. But we can't keep worrying about the men we're going to meet. It's going to work out for us. I know it is!"

The Texas heat enveloped the women as they made their way from Susan's house to the church where the dance was being held. Deborah walked with trepidation, worry etched on her brow, afraid she might faint from the oppressive heat. She fanned herself with her hand, trying to cool down as she walked beside Cassandra.

Cassandra noticed Deborah's discomfort and placed a comforting hand on her arm. "Are you all right, Deb? You look a bit pale."

Deborah forced a small smile. "Just not used to this heat, I suppose. Maybe there will be men standing around the church with giant fans, waving them back and forth to help us stay cool. I don't know that I want to meet my future husband while I'm sweating like a...I would say sweating like a pig, but that's so cliche. Sweating like a lady at a dance on a very hot evening."

Cassandra chuckled softly, her eyes twinkling. "I doubt it, but we'll survive, as we always do." She paused, glancing at Deborah thoughtfully. "Are you nervous about tonight?"

Deborah's expression shifted slightly, her eyes revealing her unease. "A little. I'm not sure I'm cut out for all this dancing and socializing but I'm trying to keep an open mind. I just hope that whoever I meet will see past my awkwardness and fear."

Cassandra squeezed her arm reassuringly. "You are more than just your fears, Deborah. Remember, tonight is for us. Don't worry about disappointing anyone. Just smile and go with it!"

Deborah nodded, grateful for Cassandra's words. As they approached the church, the strains of music drifted out into the warm evening air, mingling with the murmur of voices and laughter. The flickering lanterns cast a soft glow over the scene, creating a magical atmosphere that made Deborah's worries momentarily fade away.

The sound of laughter and chatter grew louder as they entered the church hall, where couples were already twirling around the dance floor. Cassandra gave Deborah an encouraging smile before joining the other sisters as they dispersed to mingle with the crowd.

Deborah stood on the edge of the room, feeling a combination of excitement and dread knotting in her stomach.

Chapter Three

Deborah Brown's hand trembled ever so slightly on the brass handle of the dance hall's door. She took a deep breath before stepping into the whirlwind of sights and sounds that greeted her. Her blue eyes darted around the room, looking for an anchor in the sea of faces.

"Evening, Deborah," a voice called from the corner, where some local youngsters were gathered, their laughter mingling with the clink of glasses and the shuffle of boots on wood.

"Good evening," she replied.

The church pulsed with life. Couples spun and twirled, their movements a dance of shadows and light thrown by the lanterns hanging overhead. Men tipped their hats and ladies fanned themselves, cheeks flushed with excitement or perhaps the summer heat.

Deborah's foot tapped almost imperceptibly to the beat. She watched, filled with hope and a quiet longing to be part of the joy that enveloped the room.

Amidst the twirling dresses and boisterous laughter, a figure caught Deborah's attention from across the crowded room.

Susan Dailey whispered to Deborah, " His name is Aaron Tudor—the Gentle Giant as he's fondly known," He stood by the punch bowl, his towering form a beacon amidst the sea of dancers. His smile, warm and unguarded, seemed to light up the space as his eyes met hers.

Deborah's heart fluttered like a trapped bird within her chest. She turned away quickly, her fingers reaching up to twist a lock of hair around them—a nervous habit she'd developed in place of her absent knitting needles. She felt exposed. It was as though she was missing her lifeline in this lively battlefield of social interaction.

"Nice night for dancing, isn't it?" The depth of Aaron's voice cut through the din of fiddle music and chatter, surprisingly close now.

"Y-yes, quite nice," Deborah managed to murmur, not trusting herself to lift her gaze to meet his. As if her hands had a mind of their own, they busied themselves further with her hair, coiling strands into a makeshift distraction.

"Mind if I stand here a spell? Seems cooler by the wall," Aaron said, his tone easy and devoid of any pretense. He didn't seem to notice—or chose not to comment on—Deborah's diverted eyes and fidgeting hands.

"Of course," she replied, her voice steadier than she felt. "The heat can be rather oppressive."

"I'm Aaron," he said, "Aaron Tudor." He smiled at her, his brown eyes crinkling at the corners.

"Deborah Brown," she said softly, and for a moment, she allowed herself to return his smile, finding comfort in the simple exchange. It was a start, a tiny step toward something new.

Aaron edged closer. "Deborah, would you honor me with a dance?"

Her heart fluttered like a trapped bird beneath her ribs. She glanced up at him, his height casting an imposing figure, yet his smile was nothing but warm and inviting. "I-I'd be delighted," Deborah stammered.

"Excellent!" Aaron's eyes lit up, and he offered his hand with the grace of a man who knew the strength he possessed yet wielded it with care.

As they stepped onto the dance floor, Deborah could hardly believe the firm yet gentle grasp of his calloused fingers around hers. The music swelled, a lively tune that set boots and petticoats twirling.

"Step light now, just follow my lead," Aaron said, guiding her into the dance with an ease that was surprising with his size.

"Like this?" Deborah asked, her feet finding the rhythm as she allowed him to steer their course among the other dancers.

"Exactly like that," Aaron chuckled, and there was a twinkle in his eye that made her breath catch. They moved together through the steps.

"Seems you've done this before," Aaron mused, spinning her under his arm.

"Only in my dreams," she confessed, laughter bubbling from her lips as she returned to his embrace.

"Then let's make sure this dance is one worth dreaming about," Aaron replied, his voice carrying a promise that filled Deborah with a warmth that even the summer night couldn't rival.

Their banter flowed as effortlessly as their movements, and for those fleeting moments, Deborah found herself caught in a world where fear had no place, only the joy of being held in the gentle giant's steady arms.

With Aaron's hands guiding her through the dance, she should have felt secure, yet a tremor of unease quivered through her. Men had always been a storm cloud in her sunny sky, their intentions as murky as a swollen river after heavy rains. Aaron, however, seemed different. His grip was firm but kind, his eyes a calm harbor in the church filled with people.

"Doing all right?" Aaron asked, his voice low and steady over the din, like the rumble of distant thunder that promised rain but no tempest.

"Trying to," Deborah admitted, her gaze flitting away for a moment, only to be drawn back by the kindness she found in his.

"Take your time. There's no rush," he reassured, leading her through a gentle turn. His smile was like a lantern in the dark, illuminating the path ahead and beckoning her forward.

"Thank you," she said, feeling the knots of fear begin to loosen. Her doubts whispered that she was just a simple store clerk, a mediocre knitter at best, not someone who could hold the attention of this gentle giant.

"See? Just like walking in the rain, one step at a time," Aaron encouraged.

"Except I'm less likely to trip over my own feet in the rain," Deborah said, a small smile tugging at her lips despite her jitters.

"Then we'll call it a success if we make it through without any stumbles," Aaron replied with a chuckle.

As the music played on and the dancers spun around them, Deborah let herself get lost in the rhythm of Aaron's lead. She allowed the warmth of his hand at her back to chase away the chills of past fears, the sound of his laughter to fill the spaces where doubt used to dwell. For the first time in a long while, she felt seen for the dreams nestled within her heart. And perhaps, just maybe, those dreams included a dance or two with a man who saw her as more than average.

The fiddle music slowed to a gentle hum, and the dancers dispersed for a moment of reprieve. Deborah found herself beside Aaron at the refreshment table, her fingers lightly brushing against the lace tablecloth as she reached for a glass of punch.

"Quite the evening, ain't it?" Aaron's voice was smooth, like the worn leather reins he often handled on his ranch.

"Indeed," Deborah replied, her tone soft but steady. "I never imagined I'd be sharing a dance with... well, someone like you."

"Someone like me?" Aaron raised an eyebrow, a playful challenge in his gaze.

"Someone so..." She paused, searching for the right word that wouldn't betray her nerves. "You do realize you are a very large man, don't you?"

"Ah," he chuckled, tipping his hat back slightly. "And here I thought it was my two-stepping skills that impressed you."

Deborah couldn't help but smile, the tension easing from her shoulders. "That too," she said. "I...well, you're a bit intimidating, if you haven't noticed." She took a sip of her drink, finding courage in the sweetness.

"Think of me as one of your female friends." Aaron's grin was warm, inviting. "There's nothing to be afraid of or intimidated by."

"Thank you," she murmured, touched by his words.

"Miss Brown—Deborah," Aaron began, his voice taking on a softer timbre. "May I be forthright?"

"Please do," she answered, surprised by her own eagerness.

"I've watched you since you walked into this church, seen how you carry yourself with such grace. But it didn't look like you expected any man to approach you." He leaned in closer, his presence both imposing and comforting. "You're much more than you give yourself credit for."

Deborah's heart fluttered, vulnerable under his gaze. She wrestled with the desire to open up, to share the fears that gnawed at her. With a steadying breath, she took the plunge.

"Aaron, there's something I must confess," she said, her voice barely above a whisper. "My fear of men, it runs deep, and though you've been nothing but kind, I find myself waiting for the other boot to drop."

"Deborah," he said earnestly, "you've no cause to fear me. I'd like to prove myself worthy of your trust, however long it takes."

"Would you? Even if it meant..." She hesitated, her next words feeling like a leap off a cliff. "Even if it meant waiting to consummate our marriage until I'm ready?"

"Absolutely," Aaron responded without a hint of hesitation, his voice firm and resolute. "I want you to feel safe with me. To see that my intentions are true."

"Thank you, Aaron," she breathed, relief washing over her. For the first time, she considered the possibility of a future where her fears didn't dictate her heart's desires—a future where perhaps, love could gently unravel the tightly wound yarn of her past.

Aaron reached for Deborah's hand, his touch as reassuring as the solid earth beneath their feet. "You've got a courageous heart, Deborah. Takes a lot to speak your truth in this world."

The warmth from his grasp seemed to seep into her skin, fueling a newfound courage that fluttered in her chest. She allowed herself a small smile, nodding in silent gratitude for his understanding.

"Shall we?" he asked, gesturing back to the lively dance floor where couples were once again finding their rhythm.

"I'd like that," she replied.

As they rejoined the dance, the fiddler picked up the pace, bow dancing across strings with wild abandon. The music was infectious, and Deborah found her feet moving with more confidence, her steps matching Aaron's with surprising ease. Laughter bubbled up from her throat, genuine and free, as she spun under Aaron's arm, her skirt twirling around her.

"Look at you, dancing like you've been doing it all your life," Aaron teased gently, a glint of admiration in his eyes.

"Maybe I have," Deborah said, grinning up at him.

"Wouldn't doubt it for a second," he said, chuckling.

As the evening wore on, the heat of the summer night wrapped around them like a warm embrace, but the heat between Deborah and Aaron was of a different sort—a spark of connection that was kindling something more. They danced until her feet hurt, but she just couldn't stop. She was enjoying herself too much in this man's arms.

When the final notes of the fiddle hung in the air, they stood side by side, breathless from the dance. Aaron looked down at Deborah, his gaze sincere.

Aaron looked at her. "The way I understand it, if I'm interested in marriage, I'm supposed to ask now, and then we go and have Amos marry us."

She nodded slowly. "That's my understanding."

"Well, I'm not a man of flowery words, so I'm just going to say it. I want you to cook my breakfast in the mornings after sleeping in my arms all night. With that being the case, I guess that means we need to get married."

She laughed, but his words triggered her fear. "But we can still wait to consummate?" she asked.

He nodded. "Absolutely. I won't do anything you don't want me to do. Though..."

"Yes?"

"I sure would like it if I can kiss you now and then while you're getting used to me."

She swallowed hard, but nodded. "I suppose that makes sense."

"Let's go see Amos then. I can't wait to take you home with me."

Feeling as if she was marrying a stranger, a gentle giant no less, she followed him to the preacher, and they spoke their words quickly. When the pastor told him he could kiss her, he brushed his lips across her cheek. And that's when she knew she'd made the right decision. He really did care how she felt.

Chapter Four

Deborah perched on the edge of the buggy seat, her hands folded neatly in her lap. Beside her, Aaron sat as still as a statue, his gaze fixed on the road ahead. She let her eyes wander over to him, taking in the strong line of his jaw and the way his dark hair curled just above the collar of his shirt.

"Beautiful night, isn't it?" Aaron's voice cut through the quiet, low and steady like the roll of distant thunder.

She nodded, tucking a loose strand of brown hair behind her ear. "Yes, very." Her words were a soft-spoken whisper, betraying the whirlwind of thoughts inside her. Could she be the wife he needed? The fear gnawed at her insides, but Deborah willed herself to look beyond it, out at the vast Texas landscape unfurling before them.

The buggy wheels spun a comforting melody against the dirt road, a rhythm that seemed to say all was well. They rolled past fields dotted with wildflowers and cattle grazing beneath the relentless summer sun. The heat hung heavy in the air, but the wide-open spaces were just what she needed to feel at home.

"Never gets old, coming home," Aaron said, breaking the silence again. His brown eyes stared at the home where he'd been raised and still lived now that his parents had moved on.

"It's... overwhelming," Deborah admitted, allowing herself to voice the awe that tightened her chest.

"Give it time," Aaron replied, the corners of his mouth lifting ever so slightly. "It'll feel like home soon enough."

She hoped he was right. Deborah's trepidation mingled with a burgeoning sense of adventure. Perhaps, someday, she could find the courage to open her heart.

The carriage creaked to a halt, and Deborah's gaze fixed on the sight before her. A farmhouse, all honey-colored wood and white trim, sat nestled off the main road. It was larger than she'd expected.

"Here we are," Aaron announced with a hint of pride in his voice.

"Is this really ours?" Deborah couldn't keep the wonder from her voice as she peered out at the sprawling property that stretched out around the house.

"Every acre," he confirmed. Aaron's hand appeared to help her down. His smile gave her confidence as she placed her hand in his.

Deborah felt her heart flutter like a trapped bird at his touch. Stepping down from the buggy, her boots met the ground of what was now her home. The earth was firm and real under her feet, grounding her.

"Careful now," Aaron murmured, steadying her with gentle firmness.

"Thank you," she said, her voice barely above a whisper as she clung momentarily to his arm. She looked up at him then, and for a moment, their eyes locked—a silent exchange of mutual support.

They ascended the porch steps together, the wooden boards creaking beneath their weight. Aaron's presence was a comfort beside her.

"Feels good to be home," Aaron spoke again.

"Home," Deborah repeated, tasting the word, finding it sweet and new on her lips. She allowed herself a small, hopeful smile, her blue eyes still taking in the expanse of their shared domain. "Yes, home."

The wooden door swung open with a welcoming groan, and Deborah stepped into the heart of her new dwelling.

"Cozy, isn't it?" Aaron's voice was a low rumble behind her, rich with pride for the home he'd grown up in.

"Very," she replied, her voice steadier than she felt as she surveyed the room. There were a few lanterns spread throughout the room, and she found them welcoming. She drew closer to the light, feeling the chill of apprehension melt away in its embrace.

"Let me show you the rest." Aaron gestured with a sweep of his arm, the simple motion conveying both an invitation and a promise.

Aaron picked up two of the lanterns, and they walked together down a short hallway, the floorboards creaking beneath their steps. At the end of the corridor, he opened a door to reveal a bedroom. The bed was made neatly, a quilt of deep blues and greens folded at its foot.

"This is ours," he said, his words colored with a tenderness that wrapped around her like a warm shawl.

Deborah's hands fluttered to her chest, her fingers brushing the fabric of her dress. "It's lovely, Aaron." She wanted to ask if there was another room she could sleep in, but she felt that may be pushing her luck a bit too far. He'd been kind so far, and he'd agreed to wait for their wedding night. She couldn't possibly ask for more from him.

He stepped closer, his large hands enclosing hers. His eyes searched hers, finding the quiet storm that swirled in their depths. "I know this is all new, Deborah. We'll go slow. Step by step, day by day," he assured her.

She met his gaze, finding an anchor in his steady presence. "Thank you, Aaron. For understanding."

"Always," he promised, squeezing her hands before letting go. "This is your home now too. Together, we'll fill it with memories. Good ones."

Deborah nodded, the corners of her mouth lifting ever so slightly. Yes, memories. And perhaps, in time, love would be among them.

Deborah allowed herself a moment to believe in the future. The trepidation that had knotted her insides began to unravel, thread by thread, with every gentle word Aaron shared. She dared to look up at him, and for the first time since they met at the altar, she smiled—a small, budding thing that spoke of fragile hope.

"Thank you," she whispered. "For being so... kind."

"Nothing to thank me for," Aaron replied, his deep voice a comforting rumble in the quiet room. "We're in this together, Deborah."

IT WAS A NEW DAY, DEBORAH'S first full day as Mrs. Tudor, and as much as it daunted her, it also sparked curiosity about what lay ahead.

She dressed quickly, her fingers fumbling with the buttons of her dress, still unaccustomed to the quiet of the house. Stepping out into the hallway, the scents of coffee and something sweet baking wafted towards her. Following the fragrances like a lifeline, she found herself in the kitchen where a woman stood with her back to her, humming softly as she attended to a skillet on the stove.

"Good morning," Deborah said, hoping her voice didn't betray her nervousness.

The woman turned, revealing a kindly face framed by graying hair. "Morning, Mrs. Tudor. I'm Charlotte, the housekeeper. Mr. Aaron told me to expect you. Breakfast will be ready shortly."

"Please, just Deborah is fine," she corrected gently, taking in the sight of the bustling kitchen. "I didn't realize we had—"

"Help?" Charlotte finished for her with a knowing smile. "Mr. Aaron believes in taking good care of his land and his home. And now, of you too."

Deborah nodded, a question forming in her mind—one that tugged at the edges of her understanding of this marriage. "And what does he... What do I do here?"

"Live, dear. Just live," Charlotte answered, her eyes crinkling at the corners. "You'll find your place here. You'll see."

"Live," Deborah echoed, the word sitting strangely yet pleasantly atop her tongue. It wasn't an answer, but as she took a seat at the table and watched the sun climb higher, it felt like enough for now.

After breakfast, Deborah found Charlotte in the kitchen, her hands growing more confident as they folded dough and chopped vegetables.

"Your stew smells heavenly, dear," Charlotte praised, her voice warm like the summer breeze drifting through the open window.

"Thank you," Deborah replied, allowing herself a small smile. "Cooking always did bring me comfort."

The hours slipped by like water over river stones, smooth and steady. When Aaron returned from the fields, he entered the house with a tired satisfaction etched into his broad frame.

"Smells like heaven in here," Aaron said, his deep voice carrying easily through the homely space.

"Deborah's doing," Charlotte chimed in, setting the table for supper.

As they sat down to eat, the light-hearted chatter that had filled the day faded into a thoughtful silence. Deborah took a moment to gather her courage before looking up from her plate to meet Aaron's gaze across the table.

"Aaron," she began, her voice steady despite the fluttering in her chest, "I've been wondering... what do you expect from me? In our marriage, I mean."

He paused, setting down his fork, his brown eyes meeting hers with an honesty that touched something deep within her. "I guess I'm looking for companionship, to start. Someone to share the quiet with, the laughter too. In time, love, maybe even children. But we don't need to rush into anything. We'll take it one step at a time."

His words wrapped around her like a gentle embrace, and she felt a warmth that wasn't just from the stew in her belly. "Companionship," she repeated. "I think I'd like that very much."

"Then that's what we'll do." Aaron nodded, his smile as comforting as the familiar creak of the wooden floors beneath their feet.

IN THE PARLOR, DEBORAH spent her evening knitting a pair of socks, as she did so many nights. She could hear the steady scrape of Aaron's knife against wood.

"What are you making?" she asked, peering over at the small figure emerging from the block in his hands.

"Little rabbit," Aaron replied without pausing, his hands sure and practiced. "For the mantel, maybe."

She smiled at the thought of the wooden creature taking its place in their home. As the fire crackled in the hearth, its glow casting flickering shadows across the room, Deborah felt something warm unfurl inside her chest. Here she was, sitting with a man who had been a stranger just yesterday, sharing a silence that felt comfortable.

"Tell me about your life before... all this," she ventured, curious about the chapters that had led him to her.

Aaron glanced up, his eyes reflecting the firelight. "Well, it was mostly work. But there were some good times too, like when the cattle sold well or the rains came just when we needed them. I was raised on this ranch, and my parents moved to Missouri a few years back, leaving me to work the land."

His half-smile hinted at memories she yearned to know, and she leaned in closer, her knitting forgotten in her lap. "And now?"

"Now," he said, setting down his whittling, "I've got someone to share those good times with." He reached out, his roughened hand brushing lightly against hers.

Deborah's breath hitched at the contact, her skin tingling where his fingers met hers. She met his gaze, seeing the gentle invitation in his eyes. Then, softly, as if testing the waters of a still pond, Aaron leaned in and kissed her.

Surprise fluttered through Deborah, quickly chased by a sweetness that made her heart race. His lips were warm, the kiss tender and unhurried, speaking of patience and a promise of more to come. When they parted, she caught the faintest hint of a smile playing on his lips, mirroring the one spreading across her own.

"Goodnight, Deborah," he murmured.

"Goodnight, Aaron," she whispered back. She got to her feet and went into the bedroom, ready for sleep as well.

As she lay in bed later, the memory of the kiss lingered, a promise etched into her thoughts. She imagined more kisses, laughter shared, and the pitter-patter of little feet—a future that seemed brighter than the morning star outside her window. In the quiet darkness, Deborah realized she hadn't just married a good man. She had found a companion, a partner, and perhaps, in time, a love that would grow.

Chapter Five

The Texas sun bore down on Deborah as she hesitated outside the barn, her fingers fumbling with a strand of brown hair that had escaped her practical bun. She took a tentative step forward, only to retreat once more. This was Aaron's barn, and she had to wonder how he'd feel if she walked inside.

"Come on, Deborah," she whispered to herself. With each timid approach toward the ranch chores that awaited, memories of her past life beckoned, filled with the clinking of store bells and the soft murmur of yarn between her fingers.

Deborah's blue eyes, usually calm pools reflecting her inner tranquility, now shimmered with the glaze of homesickness as she thought of Cassie. Oh, how she missed those long afternoons spent in the comforting embrace of her best friend's laughter, the way Cassie could turn any chore into a moment of joy. Together, they had weathered the uncertainty. Without her, Deborah felt alone.

She longed for the simple routines, the easy camaraderie shared with her sisters in the cozy rooms of their childhood home, where every creak of the floorboards was familiar, every window framed with the delicate curtains they had sewn together.

"Nothing's right," Deborah murmured, the sound barely carrying beyond the confines of her parched lips. She pictured Cassie's knowing smile, imagined her gentle nudge pushing Deborah beyond the comfort of knitting needles and into the unknown ranch life.

"Hey, just take it one day at a time," Cassie would say. But Cassie's voice felt miles away now, and the weight of solitude pressed heavily upon Deborah's slender shoulders.

With a sigh, she picked up a small bucket meant for feeding the chickens. As she walked toward the coop, she couldn't help but feel that maybe, just maybe, this new world could one day feel like home too.

Deborah hesitated at the threshold of the chicken coop. Her gaze drifted over the vast expanse of Aaron's land, each acre unfamiliar and daunting. She could almost hear the chickens clucking impatiently, but it was another sound that caught her attention—a set of heavy footsteps approaching from behind.

"Mind if I join you?" The deep voice was tinged with warmth.

She turned to see Aaron striding toward her. A soft smile tugged at the corners of her lips, a reflex she didn't know she still possessed.

"Of course not," Deborah replied. "I'm afraid I'm not much good with chickens."

Aaron's chuckle rumbled through the air, disarming in its sincerity. "Well, you're in luck. Chickens happen to be one of my specialties."

Together, they walked into the coop, the hens scattering with flaps and feathers. Aaron reached down and expertly scooped up a handful of feed, scattering it with practiced ease. Deborah had always been on cleaning duty back at the foundling home. It was rare for her to be sent out to care for any of the animals.

"See? Just like this," he said, gently guiding her hand to mimic his. "They're just hungry is all."

"Everything here is so... different," she confided, finding courage in his steady gaze.

"New beginnings often are," he mused, leaning against the wooden fence. "But you're not alone, Deborah. Remember that."

"Sometimes it feels that way," she admitted. "Back home, I knew who I was. Here, I feel like a piece of a puzzle that doesn't quite fit."

"Give it time," Aaron encouraged. "You'll find your place here, I promise. Texas has a way of growing on you."

"Did it grow on you?" Deborah asked, her curiosity piqued.

"Born and raised under this big old sky," Aaron said, sweeping his arm across the horizon. "But even I had to find my footing when I took over the ranch. It's not about the land, Deborah. It's about the life you build on it."

"Life seems so..." She paused, searching for the right words. "Big here."

"Big can be good. Means there's room to grow. And I hope we'll do just that. Together."

"Thank" —she swallowed against the lump in her throat— "thank you, Aaron."

"Anytime," he replied with a nod, his gentle giant reputation evident in the kindness of his actions.

As they finished with the chickens, Deborah felt a tiny seed of hope taking root within her. Perhaps, with Aaron by her side, she could learn to navigate this vast new world. And maybe, just maybe, she could call it home.

DEBORAH SAT ON THE porch steps, the wooden planks warm beneath her as the late afternoon sun dipped toward the horizon. She watched Aaron stride across the yard, a lasso coiled in his hand and a wide-brimmed hat shielding his eyes from the waning light. He caught her gaze and tipped his hat with a smile.

"Evening, Deborah. How about a quick lesson before supper?" he called out.

"Lesson in what?" she asked, a flutter of nerves in her belly.

"Roping. You never know when it might come in handy," Aaron replied with a chuckle.

She hesitated, but his encouraging nod coaxed her to her feet. The rope felt strange and heavy in her hands, but with Aaron's patient guidance, she began to mimic his movements. Loop by loop, her throws improved, and each time the lasso landed closer to the target—a fence post patiently playing the part of a steer.

"Look at that! You're a natural." Aaron's praise was genuine, and she felt a swell of pride.

"Thank you, Aaron. It's... nice to feel useful," Deborah said, the words coming easier than they used to.

"More than useful. You're part of this ranch now," he assured her.

Later, under the soft glow of the oil lamp, Deborah's fingers worked the knitting needles with practiced ease. The rhythmic clicking was a soothing counterpoint to the chirping of the crickets outside. A pair of socks began to take shape, their pattern familiar and comforting.

"Knitting again?" Aaron's voice was soft as he joined her on the porch.

"Always helps me think," Deborah admitted without looking up.

"What're you thinking about?" he asked, leaning back in his chair with a creak of wood.

"Home. Family. How things change," she said, a wistful note in her voice.

"Change can be good," Aaron offered, reaching over to gently touch the emerging sock. "Like these socks. Warm, dependable. Like you."

Deborah met his gaze then, her blue eyes shining in the lamplight. "Dependable is a nice thing to be," she mused.

"Best thing," Aaron agreed. "Means you can count on something. Or someone."

"Like counting on the sun to rise," she added, the corners of her mouth lifting in a small, contented smile.

"Exactly like that," Aaron affirmed.

In the quiet companionship, Deborah found an unexpected sense of peace. For the first time since arriving in Texas, she felt her old and new lives intertwining. It was a comforting thought.

THE DUSTY PATH TO THE neighboring ranch was a far cry from the well-trodden roads back home, and Deborah couldn't help but feel a flutter of nervousness in her belly. Beside her, Aaron walked with an ease that came from years of striding across these lands, his boots kicking up little clouds behind him.

"I just want to spend a minute visiting the Daileys," he said, a twinkle in his eye. "No matter when you stop by there, they always have some kind of sweet treat waiting, so I try to stop by often."

Deborah managed a shy smile, her hands clasped together in front of her simple cotton dress. She had yet to meet most of their neighbors, and the thought both excited and unnerved her.

"Sounds lovely," she murmured.

Aaron glanced at her, noticing her tension, and slowed his pace to match hers more closely. "You'll fit right in, Deb. Just be your sweet self."

When they arrived, Susan, Elizabeth's sister, greeted them with open arms, enveloping Deborah in a hug that was surprisingly strong. The warmth of her welcome melted some of the ice around Deborah's heart.

"Come on in! I thought you two would get along well!" Susan ushered them inside, where the smell of baked goods and the sound of friendly chatter filled the air.

As the afternoon wore on, Deborah found herself swept into the activities of the ranch. She helped collect eggs from the chicken coop, laughing softly when a hen pecked gently at her hand, and the others praised her for being a natural.

"See? You're a proper rancher's wife now," Aaron said, pride evident in his voice.

The following Sunday, as the church bell rang clear through the morning air, Deborah felt the gentle squeeze of Aaron's hand as they stepped inside. Her sisters were there, all smiles and Sunday dresses. Cassie, with her warm brown eyes, rushed forward and wrapped Deborah in an embrace.

"Missed you every day," Cassie whispered, holding on tight.

"Me too," Deborah replied, her voice thick with emotion. They pulled back, and she saw the understanding in Cassie's gaze.

As days turned into, Deborah's initial trepidation gave way to a quiet confidence. She learned the names of the ranch hands, could saddle a horse with practiced ease, and her laughter became a common melody that mingled with the wind.

"Never thought I'd see the day when I'd wake up excited to mend fences," Deborah confessed one evening as they sat on the porch, watching the sun dip below the horizon.

"Life has a funny way of surprising us," Aaron replied, his hand finding hers in the dimming light.

"Surprising and wonderful," she added, her blue eyes reflecting the last rays of sunlight.

"Exactly," Aaron agreed, and in his steady gaze, Deborah found the sense of belonging and security she had longed for since arriving in Texas.

THE SUN CLIMBED HIGH, casting a sweltering blanket over the vast expanse of Aaron's ranch. Deborah stood beside him, a rifle cradled awkwardly in her arms as she squinted at the row of tin cans arranged on the fence post.

"Steady now," Aaron said. "Just like I showed you. Breathe easy."

Deborah nodded, trying to mimic the quiet assurance that seemed to come so naturally to him. She could feel the weight of the rifle, an unfamiliar pressure against her shoulder, and the heat of the Texas sun pressing down upon them both.

"All right." Her voice was more a whisper than she intended, a stark contrast to the hum of activity that buzzed around the ranch. She took a deep breath, letting it out slowly as Aaron had instructed, and squeezed the trigger.

The blast was louder than she expected, making her jump despite her preparations. To her astonishment, one of the cans clattered to the ground, and she turned to Aaron, her eyes wide with surprise.

"Look at that! You got it!" His face broke into a broad grin, the pride in his voice wrapping around her like a warm embrace.

"Did I really?" The disbelief in her tone matched the fluttering in her chest—a mix of excitement and newfound confidence.

"Sure as the sky is blue," he chuckled, and there was that nurturing warmth again, the kind that made the ranch feel less daunting, more like a place she might one day call home.

She let out a soft, disbelieving laugh, feeling a strange sense of accomplishment. With each passing day, under Aaron's patient guidance, Deborah found herself tackling tasks she'd never imagined possible. Her hands, once reserved for knitting and folding clothes at the General Store, were now calloused from reins and rope. And here she was, shooting tin cans off a fence like some Wild West sharpshooter.

"Again?" Aaron asked, gesturing to the remaining cans with a tilt of his head.

"Again," Deborah agreed, the word feeling like a promise. She steadied herself, aiming with more confidence this time. The gunshot rang out, another can toppled, and she couldn't help the smile that spread across her face.

"Seems you're full of surprises, Mrs. Tudor," Aaron teased gently, reloading the rifle for her.

"Maybe I am," Deborah replied, a playful note in her voice that felt foreign yet fitting. She glanced up at Aaron, their eyes meeting. There was a flicker of something there—an acknowledgment of her growth, of the partnership they were building together.

"Let's finish off those cans," Aaron suggested, and Deborah nodded, eager to continue. As she focused on the target, she realized it wasn't just about hitting cans. It was about hitting her stride in this new life, one shot at a time.

DEBORAH'S FINGERS TRAILED along the rough wooden fence, her gaze following the sprawling horizon that painted a canvas of endless possibilities. She paused, leaning against the sturdy barrier, and let out a contented sigh.

"Beautiful, isn't it?" Aaron's voice came from behind, his presence as reassuring as the land itself.

"More than I ever imagined," Deborah admitted, turning to face him. His eyes held a glint of pride as they rested on her.

"Seems like you're taking to ranch life like a duck to water."

She chuckled, thinking back to her first tentative steps on this soil, "Feels like home now, thanks to you."

"Ah, it's all you, Deb. You've made this place shine," Aaron said, closing the distance between them with a few easy strides.

A soft breeze played with strands of Deborah's hair, and she tucked them behind her ear, her blue eyes reflecting the vastness above. "I used to feel so lost in all this space. Now, it feels like...like there's room for dreams to grow."

"Always was," Aaron murmured, his hand finding hers, their fingers intertwining naturally.

"Who would have thought? Me, a rancher's wife," Deborah mused, a playful twinkle in her eye.

"Best one this side of Fort Worth," Aaron declared, giving her hand a gentle squeeze.

"You really think so?" she asked after a moment, seeking confirmation of her newfound role.

"Every word." Aaron's affirmation was as solid as the ground beneath their feet.

"Then I suppose we'll make quite the team," Deborah said.

"Already are, my dear. Already are," Aaron replied, pulling her into a gentle embrace.

Chapter Six

The Texas sun was relentless, a fiery chaperone to Jane's new beginning. Stepping onto the dusty platform, her heart hammered with a cocktail of nerves and elation. The steam from the train hissed a farewell as she gripped her suitcase—the one containing her few worldly possessions—her knuckles white with anticipation.

"Jane! Over here!" A familiar voice sliced through the throng of people.

Deborah's dress fluttered lightly in the breeze, the pattern lost in the shuffle but her smile impossible to miss. Jane's steps quickened, the ground beneath her seeming to usher her toward the open arms of family.

"I'm so glad you're here!" Deborah exclaimed, her eyes twinkling as she pulled Jane into an embrace.

"Thank you for coming to get me," Jane said, the tension leaving her shoulders as she returned the tight hug. "I can't believe I'm finally here."

"Believe it," Deborah said, holding her at arm's length now, her gaze sweeping over Jane with sisterly appraisal. "Texas suits you already."

"Does it?" Jane couldn't help but grin, feeling the truth of it in her bones. "Well, I think I'm ready for whatever it has to offer."

"Let's get you to Susan's house," Deborah said as they weaved through the crowd. They approached a buggy drawn by a pair of chestnut horses.

"Here, allow me," Deborah offered, taking Jane's suitcase and hoisting it onto the carriage with ease.

"Thank you," Jane murmured, her gaze lingering on the sturdy horses. "They're beautiful."

"Ah, those two are Bess and Duke," Deborah replied with a chuckle, patting the flank of the nearest horse affectionately. "Susan's husband David trained them for Aaron."

"They sound like nice people," Jane said, feeling a bit intimidated. "Are you sure they don't mind me staying with them?"

"You'll love them!" Deborah said, helping Jane up into the buggy. "They are truly kind people, and they have plenty of room."

As Deborah drove away from the station, they slowly left Fort Worth and moved into the rural area outside it. Open plains stretched out toward the horizon, dotted with the occasional farmhouse and wandering cattle.

A short while later, the Dailey homestead came into view. It was a modest but well-kept two-story house, with a wraparound porch that seemed to invite the world inside. On that porch, a group of women stood waiting, their forms silhouetted by the afternoon light. As the carriage drew closer, Jane could make out their expressions—eyes bright with anticipation, smiles spreading contagiously.

"Are those...?" Jane began, leaning forward for a better look.

"All of our sisters, yes," Deborah confirmed, her voice warm with pride. "They've been looking forward to this day almost as much as I have."

The buggy came to a stop, and before Jane could even step down, the women descended upon her like a flurry of summer dresses, each one eager to greet her. There were hugs and kisses on cheeks, laughter mingling with the buzz of excited chatter. Jane found herself swept up in the whirlwind of affection, every embrace banishing a bit more of her uncertainty.

"Welcome home, Jane!" they chorused, and the words seemed to bloom in her chest like wildflowers after a rain.

"Home," Jane whispered, a smile finding its way onto her lips.

"Jane, I've missed you!" Imogene said, spreading her arms for a hug from Jane.

"Imogene," Jane said, running into the embrace of the sister she was closest to. "I can't believe I'm finally here."

"Believe it, sister. Texas is ready for you," Imogene replied, her eyes glistening with unshed tears.

"Is it always this warm?" Jane asked with a laugh that tumbled into their reunion like a playful breeze.

"It's August. Thankfully, this is the hottest it gets," Susan Dailey said, fanning her face with her hand, and laughter bubbled up among them.

"Tell us everything, Jane. The train, the journey—leave nothing out!" Brenda urged, pulling Jane toward the settee.

"Was it terribly crowded? Did you meet any interesting characters?" Amy said.

"Nothing too wild," Jane said with a chuckle. "Though a gentleman did try to explain the entire history of cattle ranching to me."

"Sounds about right," Deborah muttered, smiling softly.

They gathered around Jane, their conversation flowing as easily as the river outside. Stories were traded, laughter shared, and with every word spoken, the bond between them strengthened.

"Texas does seem quite different from what I'm used to," Jane admitted, her voice tinged with excitement.

"Give it time. It'll soon feel like you've been here all your life," Deborah assured her, squeezing Jane's hand gently.

"Isn't it cozy?" Susan remarked, noticing Jane's wide-eyed appraisal. "We spend most of our evenings here, sharing stories."

"Let me show you your room," Susan said, guiding her up the narrow staircase lined with worn carpet.

The room Susan presented to Jane was small but filled with touches that transformed it from mere sleeping quarters to a sanctuary. The bed, adorned with a patchwork quilt, promised restful nights, while a simple wooden desk awaited letters yet to be penned.

"Look at that view," Jane whispered, stepping closer to the window.

"Texas has a way of getting into your heart," Susan replied, standing beside her. "You'll see. This land is part of us now."

"Thank you, Susan," Jane said, her voice catching with emotion. "For everything."

"You're not just a guest here, Jane. You're family," Susan stated firmly, placing a reassuring hand on her shoulder. "This is your home now."

"Family," Jane repeated, allowing the weight of the word to settle in her heart. As she looked out at the vast Texas landscape, she knew that this was where her future would unfold—one day, one experience at a time.

The clatter of dishes and the rich aroma of stewed beef mingled in the air as Jane stepped into the bustling kitchen. Susan ushered her towards the large wooden table where a feast spread out like a patchwork quilt of colors and textures. The room echoed with the chatter of women, their laughter rising and falling like a melody.

"Come on, sit here by me," Deborah beckoned, patting the chair beside her.

"Deborah, tell me about Texas," Jane said softly, turning to her sister. "Does it ever feel like home to you?"

"Every day, a little more," Deborah replied, her voice low, as if divulging a secret. "There's beauty in the area. Like you can breathe easier here."

"Is it as grand as they say?" Jane asked, her eyes wide with wonder.

"Grand doesn't quite cover it," Deborah chuckled, her gaze meeting Jane's with a warmth that spoke volumes. "It's like the land stretches on forever, just waiting for our dreams to catch up."

"Sounds perfect for new beginnings," Jane murmured, her spoon pausing midway to her mouth.

"Exactly." Deborah nodded, her blue eyes reflecting a quiet hope. "New beginnings for us all. You'll find a good man here. We all have."

"Thank you," Jane smiled, her heart swelling with gratitude and anticipation for the future that awaited her.

All too soon, Deborah had to head home to fix supper for Aaron. She hugged Jane goodbye as she drove the buggy back to her house.

"Jane's laughter is like music," she mused quietly. The presence of her younger sister had been so nice, soothing the homesickness that occasionally flared up.

She pulled up into the yard of the home she shared with Aaron, and set the brake on the buggy as Aaron had taught her before heading into the house.

A sense of peace enveloped her, borne from the camaraderie, the shared meal, and the stories that wove them all together.

"Even the way she sees things," Deborah continued to herself, remembering Jane's wide-eyed wonder at the Texas landscape, "makes it all seem new again."

When she reached her house, the warm glow from within promised comfort and security. Aaron was there, his tall frame casting a long shadow against the light as he stood in the doorway, waiting for her.

"Evening, Deborah," he greeted her with his deep, soothing voice, the corners of his eyes crinkling in a smile. "How was your gathering? Did Jane get in safely?"

"Full of joy," Deborah replied. She looked up at him, her blue eyes shining with unspoken gratitude. "Jane's here, the last of the ten. It feels... complete now."

"Good to hear." Aaron nodded, leaning against the wooden doorframe. "More family means stronger roots. Texas needs strong roots."

"I guess it does," she agreed. "And maybe I needed Jane more than I knew. She reminds me that we're not just surviving out here—we're living."

"Sounds like she's got the right idea," Aaron remarked, his tone lighthearted yet sincere. "You always did say family brings out the best in us."

"True enough," Deborah said, her spirit lighter than when she'd left. She glanced back at the open prairie, feeling the truth of her words settle in her heart. "True enough."

"Sounds like you've got some stories to share," Aaron said, stepping aside to let her pass into their home.

"Plenty," she replied, moving past him. "But they can wait."

"Can they now?" His voice was a low rumble, teasing yet affectionate, as he closed the door behind them and turned to face her.

"Yes," Deborah confirmed, her lips curving into a smile. The simplicity of their life together, the quiet understanding and shared dreams, filled her with a profound sense of contentment.

In the dim light of the parlor, she could see the flicker of the oil lamp reflecting in his eyes, those steady pools that had so often looked upon her with tenderness and strength. She reached out, her fingers brushing against the fabric of his shirt, feeling the solid reality of him beneath her touch.

"Deborah," Aaron murmured, his hands finding her waist, drawing her closer until there was no space left between them. His breath was warm on her cheek, and she tilted her face upward, anticipation tingling through her veins.

"Thank you, Aaron," she whispered, her words barely audible. "For making Texas feel like home."

"I..." he began, but whatever he intended to say was lost as she stood on her tiptoes and pressed her lips to his. The kiss deepened. It was a passionate affirmation of all they had built together.

He responded with equal fervor, his arms tightening around her as if he could pull her inside him.

"More kin means stronger roots," Aaron had said, and in the sanctity of their embrace, she knew it to be true. He made her feel at home, and so did her sisters.

Chapter Seven

Deborah gazed out at the vast expanse of the Texas ranch. The sun was relentless in its scorching embrace. She let out a slow breath, willing her heart to quiet its rapid beating. Standing there, with the endless horizon stretching before her, Deborah felt both insignificant and emboldened.

"Each day is a step," she murmured to herself. She had married into this life, yes, but she'd be darned if she didn't learn to love it.

With a gentle sigh, Deborah retreated into the sanctuary of the house, where a different kind of landscape awaited her. Here, in the cozy confines of the living room, balls of yarn and knitting needles lay scattered on the table.

She picked up the needles, the familiar weight of them grounding her. The yarn, which she'd dyed a soft shade of lilac, looped over her fingers. Knitting wasn't just a pastime for her. It was a lifeline, each stitch a tiny victory woven from strands of courage.

Deborah began to knit. Her movements were rhythmic, almost meditative, as she watched the pattern come alive under her touch. Each loop was a small triumph over the doubts that plagued her, over the fear that she would never truly belong.

"Simple stitches," she whispered, finding comfort in the repetition, "like simple days."

The heat of the summer seemed to melt away, each row building upon the last, a tangible representation of her growing confidence. With every completed sock, she was not only warming the toes of her family and friends but also stitching together the fabric of her new existence.

"Knitting is like ranching, I think," Deborah thought, a smile playing on her lips. "A bit of patience, a lot of hard work, and before you know it, something beautiful comes out of it all."

In the loops and knots of her handiwork, Deborah found solace. And with each passing day, as her hands danced with wool, her heart grew more entwined with the land and the life she was determined to build.

DEBORAH'S LAUGHTER mingled with her sisters' as the trio sat around the wooden kitchen table, each immersed in her own craft. Sunbeams slipped through the curtains, casting a warm glow on their work. Deborah's fingers nimbly maneuvered the knitting needles, while Faith's hands were buried in colorful fabric patches, piecing together a quilt. Hannah's nimble fingers were busy crocheting delicate lace.

"Remember when Paul tried to fix the roof himself?" Hannah asked, her voice dancing with mirth.

"Nearly scared Mrs. Jackson to death hanging off the edge like that!" Faith chimed in, glancing up from her quilt with a grin.

Deborah smiled, the memory brightening her eyes. "I think he learned his lesson. Never did it again."

Their shared laughter filled the room, a sweet symphony of familial comfort that cushioned Deborah's lingering insecurities. Here, among her sisters, she felt her spirits lifted, her resolve strengthened by their easy camaraderie and mutual understanding.

The screen door creaked open, and Aaron stepped inside, his large frame momentarily blocking the sunlight. He paused at the pump, drawing water into a tin cup with practiced ease. His presence was like a gentle wave, unfurling across the room to wash over them without disrupting the harmony of the sisters' gathering.

"Good afternoon, ladies," Aaron greeted them, his voice deep but carrying a softness that matched the tender look in his brown eyes.

"Hello, Aaron!" Faith said cheerily, her eyes crinkling with affection.

"Care to join us?" Hannah teased lightly, gesturing to an empty chair with her embroidery hoop.

"Wouldn't miss it for the world," he replied with an easy smile, setting the cup down and pulling up a chair to sit with them. "I see the blanket's coming along nicely, Faith. And Hannah, that lace is beautiful. I'd love to see Deborah wear a dress with that around the collar."

"Thank you, Aaron," Hannah responded, her cheeks coloring with pleasure at the compliment.

Deborah watched him, noting how effortlessly he blended into their little circle, his laughter joining theirs. She marveled at how someone so strong could carry such gentleness within him, a thought that warmed her more than the summer heat outside.

"Deborah's making another pair of socks," Martha offered, nodding toward Deborah's knitting. "She says it's nothing special, but we all know better."

"Nothing special." Aaron shook his head, casting an appreciative glance at the emerging pattern. "Your skill is plain to see, Deborah. It's in every stitch."

"Thank you, Aaron," Deborah murmured, a blush creeping up her neck. The simple praise from this gentle giant stirred something within her, a sense of pride she wasn't used to feeling.

"Besides," Aaron continued, his gaze meeting hers with an earnest intensity, "it's the simple things that make life out here. A good pair of socks can make all the difference on a cold morning."

"True enough," Deborah conceded, a soft chuckle escaping her lips. As she settled back into the rhythm of her knitting, her heart swelled with gratefulness—for her sisters, for Aaron, and for the new life she was crafting, one day and one stitch at a time.

Aaron turned to Deborah, a twinkle in his eye. "Would you like to learn more about ranch life, Deborah? I could show you a thing or two about caring for the animals."

Deborah hesitated for a moment, her knitting needles pausing mid-stitch. She glanced at her sisters, who nodded encouragingly. "I'd like that," she said, her voice soft but steady.

"Great!" Aaron's smile widened. "We'll start in the morning!"

AS AARON LED DEBORAH out the door, the screen slammed shut behind them. They walked side by side to the barn, a gentle breeze carrying the scent of hay and horses their way.

"Each horse has a personality, just like people," Aaron explained as they entered the cool, dim interior of the barn. He pointed to a chestnut mare with a white blaze on her forehead. "That's Molly. She's gentle as a lamb. And over there is Daisy. She's spirit, but he's reliable."

As they approached Molly, Deborah's gaze lingered on the animal's large, soulful eyes. Aaron fetched a brush from the nearby shelf and handed it to her. "It's all about being gentle and firm," he instructed.

"Like this?" Deborah tentatively ran the brush along Molly's flank, her hands guided by Aaron's firm yet kind grasp.

"Exactly like that," Aaron praised. "You're a natural, Deborah."

She felt a flutter of happiness at his words, and a newfound confidence began to take root within her. Her fingers moved more assuredly now, her strokes smooth and rhythmic.

"Does it feel good, Molly?" Deborah asked softly, rewarded with a contented nicker from the mare. Aaron chuckled beside her, the sound both reassuring and heartening.

"Seems like she approves," he said, and Deborah couldn't help but smile, her earlier insecurities melting away under the quiet companionship of the horse and the patient man beside her.

"Thank you, Aaron," she said, grateful for the simple joy of the moment, her heart light with the promise of many such lessons to come.

DEBORAH FOLLOWED AARON out to where the fence line began its zigzag pattern across the ranch. She squinted against the sunlight, feeling the heat of summer on her skin.

"Here we are," Aaron said, pointing toward a section of fence that had seen better days. "Storm last week took a toll on these old boards."

"Looks like quite the job," Deborah commented, examining the sagging posts and splintered wood.

"Nothing we can't handle." Aaron's confidence was contagious, and Deborah found herself nodding, rolling up the sleeves of her simple dress.

"All right then, show me what to do."

Aaron selected a hammer from his toolbox and handed it to her along with a fistful of nails. "We'll start by replacing the loose boards. Just aim true and hit the nail square on the head."

Deborah positioned a nail against the weathered wood, took a deep breath, and swung. The first strike was hesitant, barely grazing the metal, but Aaron didn't criticize. Instead, he offered an encouraging nod. "Steady now, you'v got this."

Her second attempt sang with the satisfying thud of the hammer connecting solidly. The nail drove in straight, securing the board back into place.

"Look at that! You're a quick study, Deborah," Aaron praised, his eyes crinkling in the corners with genuine admiration.

"Thank you," she replied, feeling a swell of pride. Her hands, nimble from years of knitting, were proving just as adept with a hammer and nails. It was odd how he made her feel as if she was more than mediocre when no one else in her life had ever been able to.

As they moved along the fence line, the rhythm of their work harmonized with the sounds of the ranch—the distant lowing of cattle, the rustle of the wind through the grass. Aaron shared tales of his life as a rancher, each story woven with humor and a wisdom born of experience.

"Once had a calf born right in the middle of a downpour. Named him Stormy. Turned out to be one of the best bulls we ever raised," Aaron recounted, chuckling at the memory.

"Sounds like quite the character," Deborah said, smiling as she imagined the scene.

"Every animal here has a story," Aaron continued. "Just like every person. That's what makes this place special. It's not just land and livestock—it's history and heart."

"History and heart," Deborah repeated softly, liking the sound of it. She could see that now, the way the ranch held its own kind of romance.

"Exactly. And now, you're becoming a part of that story, too."

Deborah glanced at Aaron, his profile strong against the expansive sky. There was a gentleness to him that was in direct contrast to his rugged appearance, a kindness that made her feel safe and cherished.

"Thanks for sharing this with me, Aaron. For teaching me," she said, her voice carrying the weight of her gratitude.

"Anytime, Deborah. It's a pleasure to see you find your place here." His smile was like an unspoken promise, one of many lessons and shared moments to come.

DEBORAH AND AARON MADE their way back to the house. Dust clung to her dress, and Deborah's hands felt rough from the day's labor, but within her chest, there was an unfamiliar lightness—a sense of accomplishment that swelled with every step she took alongside Aaron.

"Let me see when supper will be ready," Deborah offered as they entered the house, her voice carrying that new-found confidence.

"Much obliged," Aaron replied, his deep voice resonating in the quiet space.

She returned a moment later. "Charlotte said it's all ready, and she was just waiting for us."

Once supper was on the table, they began their meal. Deborah was shocked at how tired she was. "Thank you for today," Deborah said, breaking the comfortable silence. "For being so patient with me."

Aaron's smile creased the corners of his eyes. "You're doing just fine, Deborah. It's nice to have someone to share the work with. Other than the ranch hands, of course. None of them look half as pretty as you do while pounding nails."

Her heart fluttered at his words, the simple praise sounding like poetry to her ears. She looked down at her stew, suddenly aware of how their shared endeavors had woven a thread between them, one that tightened with each passing moment.

"Feels like I'm finally getting the hang of this ranch life," she continued, her spoon tracing circles in the broth. "Never thought I'd be mending fences or grooming horses."

"Never underestimate yourself," Aaron advised, his tone gentle. "You've got more strength than you realize."

"Guess I'm full of surprises," Deborah quipped, a shy smile playing on her lips.

"You are," he agreed, his brown eyes twinkling with mirth.

They ate, laughter and soft conversation filling the gaps where silence lingered. The meal was simple, but it tasted like victory, like a small triumph in a world that demanded so much of them.

"NEVER SAW MYSELF AS a rancher's wife," Deborah murmured to herself, staring out the window at the expanse of land. "But here I am."

She turned away from the window, her gaze falling on the knitting project splayed across her chair. The yarn was a rich blue. Deborah picked up where she left off, the pattern coming to life beneath her fingers. Knit, purl, knit, purl—the rhythm was meditative, a familiar dance of creating and mending.

"Look at you," Deborah whispered to herself, a hint of laughter touching her voice. "From doubting to doing. Who would've thought?"

"Seems like those fences weren't the only things we mended today," she said softly, allowing herself a small smile.

She was no longer just Deborah Brown of the General Store. She was Deborah Tudor, the woman who could ride alongside her husband, cook a hearty meal, and share in the laughter and labor that came with ranch living.

"Tomorrow's a new day," she concluded, laying the needles aside and holding up her work to admire.

Placing the knitting gently on the chair, Deborah stretched and walked back to the window. The first stars were peeking out, and she knew that somewhere among them lay the promise of days filled with more learning, more growing, and more loving.

"Goodnight, world," she whispered. "See you in the morning."

Chapter Eight

Deborah cracked eggs into the cast-iron skillet. Aaron Tudor sat at the wooden table, a mug of steaming coffee warming his large hands. He watched her with an affectionate gaze that seemed to wrap around her like a comforting shawl. It was Charlotte's day off, so Deborah would do all the cooking.

"Smells delicious," he remarked, his deep voice filling the small kitchen.

"Almost ready," Deborah replied, the corners of her mouth lifting ever so slightly. She moved with ease around the kitchen, her simple dress swaying with each step.

They ate their breakfast in companionable silence. It was a simple morning ritual, yet it held the weight of shared dreams and quiet contentment.

After the meal, they put on their hats and stepped outside, ready for the day's hard work under the relentless Texas sun.

"Deborah," Aaron called out suddenly, holding something behind his back as she was about to head toward the chicken coop.

She turned, curiosity lighting her blue eyes. Aaron revealed a bouquet of wildflowers, their colors vibrant against the dusty backdrop of the ranch. "Picked these for you," he said, a shy smile tugging at his lips.

Deborah's heart fluttered like the wings of a butterfly caught in the morning breeze. She reached out, her fingers brushing against his as she took the flowers. "They're beautiful, Aaron. Thank you."

"Figured they'd brighten up the house some," he replied, his brown eyes crinkling at the edges. "And they remind me of you—strong and beautiful."

Her cheeks warmed, a soft blush spreading across her fair skin. "You're too kind," she said, lowering her gaze as she blushed.

"Truth is simple, Deborah. And it's just us here, no need for fancy words," Aaron said, watching her with a tenderness that continued to surprise her.

"You always know what to say," Deborah said, lifting her eyes to meet his briefly before turning away to hide her smile.

"Come on," Aaron said, gesturing toward the fields with a nod. "Let's get to work. That cow isn't going to milk herself."

Deborah followed, tucking one of the wildflowers behind her ear—a small token of the love growing as steadily as the calves that were born in the spring.

Later, Deborah wiped her brow and glanced over at Aaron, who was wrestling with an obstinate fence post. She couldn't help but admire the way his muscles flexed beneath his sweat-stained shirt as he worked.

"Break time?" she called out, her voice carrying on the warm breeze.

Aaron looked up, shielding his eyes from the sun with a broad hand, and nodded. "Sounds like a plan."

They found refuge under a grand old oak tree that had stood sentinel over the land for generations. Its wide branches offered a canopy of shade, and they settled into the cool grass, the earth grounding them after the morning's toil. Deborah leaned back against the rough bark, a sigh escaping her lips as she relished the brief respite. She offered him a jar of water and some cookies from the small basket she'd carried with her.

"Sometimes, I think about what it'll be like," she began, staring up through the leaves at slivers of blue sky. "This place filled with laughter and little feet running around."

Aaron turned to her, his expression softening. The dream of family life had been etched in his heart for so long, it felt like part of him. "That'd be something," he said, his deep voice threaded with emotion.

"Children playing hide and seek behind this very tree," Deborah continued, her gaze meeting his. She saw the spark in his eyes, the same one that ignited every time they spoke of a future together.

"Teaching them to ride, watching them grow strong and true..." Aaron's voice trailed off as he pictured the scene, the corners of his mouth lifting into a smile that mirrored Deborah's.

"Strong like their father," Deborah added, reaching out to brush a blade of grass from his leg.

"And kind-hearted like their mother." Aaron captured her hand in his, his rough skin a contrast to her delicate fingers.

Deborah blushed at his words, feeling a warmth that had little to do with the Texas heat. Here, under the protection of the oak, dreams felt within reach, as tangible as the earth beneath them and the sky above. They sat in comfortable silence, side by side, each lost in visions of a shared future that seemed to stretch out as endless and promising as the horizon.

Aaron plucked a blade of grass, twirling it between his fingers. "What do you think about 'Samuel' for a boy?" he asked with a playful glint in his eyes.

"Samuel," Deborah repeated, considering the name. She tilted her head to the side, a smile tugging at the corner of her mouth. "It's strong, but what if he's a dreamer? Maybe 'Elijah' suits a dreamer better."

"Ah, 'Elijah,'" Aaron chuckled. "He'd be the one to wander off, chasing butterflies and getting lost in thought."

"Exactly," Deborah said with a laugh, nudging him gently with her shoulder. "And for a girl, how about 'Persephone'? It has a certain elegance to it."

"Persephone would be queen of this ranch before she could even walk," Aaron agreed, nodding. "But I think 'Maggie' would be right there beside her, trying to outdo her at every turn."

"Maggie," Deborah mused aloud. "She'd have your strength and my stubbornness."

"Wouldn't stand a chance against her then," he replied with a hearty laugh that resonated through the quiet of the open land.

As their laughter faded, Aaron's gaze drifted across the fields to the small building nestled among the cottonwoods. "That schoolhouse over yonder," he began, voice tinged with nostalgia, "I learned my letters and numbers there. Mrs. Kline, she had a way of making every book feel like an adventure waiting to unfold."

"Must've been quite the sight, you at a school desk," Deborah teased, picturing the gentle giant as a boy.

"Let's just say the desks weren't quite ready for someone of my... stature," he said with a grin. "But I think our little ones will fit right in."

"Learning and growing," she smiled softly, imagining a brood of little ones with Aaron's kind eyes and her quick wit.

"Yep, learning and growing," he echoed, his heart full at the thought. "Just like we are, every day."

"Imagine it," Deborah said, her voice carrying a note of wonder. "Our children will chase the same butterflies I did, and learn from the same books you loved."

Aaron followed her line of sight, his eyes softening at the corners. "I can see them now, heads bent over slates, brows furrowed in concentration."

"Or maybe giggling behind Mrs. Kline's back when she's not looking," Deborah added with a smile that reached her sparkling blue eyes.

"Sure as the sun rises, they'll be doing both," he chuckled. "But they'll have each other, just like we do."

They sat in companionable silence for a moment, the future stretching out before them like the vast Texas plains. Then, Aaron turned to look at the ranch, his home, their future.

"Deborah, this land is more than just dirt and grass," he began, gesturing towards the expanse of their property. "It's a place for us, for our children. A shelter from storms and a cradle for dreams."

She nodded, understanding. "A place where neighbors can come for a cup of sugar or a helping hand. We'll make it thrive, Aaron. It'll be hard work, but we'll do it together."

"Hard work never scared me," Aaron said, reaching for her hand. "Especially when it's for something worth every drop of sweat and every callus."

"Every sunrise will see our dedication," Deborah promised, her voice firm despite its softness. "And every sunset will remind us why we're doing it."

"Growing a place full of love and open doors," he agreed, giving her hand an affectionate squeeze.

"Open doors," she repeated, leaning into him. "For friends, for family, for anyone in need."

THAT EVENING, DEBORAH plucked at the hem of her apron, her gaze wandering over the sprawling land that stretched before their porch.

"Imagine, Aaron," she said, her voice a soft murmur carried on the breeze, "a table right here under this very elm, all spread with my best linens."

Aaron leaned against the porch railing, his broad shoulders casting a long shadow. He watched her with an easy smile, the corners of his eyes crinkling in mirth.

"Full of your lemon cakes and berry pies, I reckon?" he teased, already picturing the scene she described.

"Exactly. Though I'll leave the pies to Amy. No one can make pies like hers," Deborah said. "And little sandwiches. Afternoons spent laughing and sharing stories with my sisters...and the ladies from church too."

"Sounds like heaven," Aaron said with a chuckle. His gaze drifted to the open fields where cattle grazed lazily. "Speaking of growing, I been thinking about the herd. We ought to bring in more heads, maybe some sturdy draft horses."

"More animals?" Deborah's eyebrows rose, but her lips curved in a pleased smile. "That means more work, Aaron. Can we manage?"

"Sure as the sun sets in the west." Aaron's voice was steady, brimming with confidence. "We'll build up the barn, get it fixed good as new. We need strong roots, Deb, for us and for the children."

"Speaking of the children..." she said softly. Her hands paused, resting on her abdomen as if feeling the stirrings of future life. She imagined children playing amidst the livestock, learning the value of hard work and community. "Maybe it's time we got started trying to make one."

Aaron looked at her, and she was a bit startled by the intensity of his gaze. "Really?" he asked. "You think you're ready?"

"Well, I do sleep in the same bed with you every night, and you haven't tried to murder me yet."

"That's true... I'm so glad I resisted those impulses." He winked at her, and she giggled softly.

Aaron wrapped his arms around Deborah, pulling her close against the warmth of his chest. Their hearts beat a shared rhythm, steady as the land beneath their feet. She tilted her face up, meeting his gaze, her green eyes reflecting the vast sky above them.

"Deb," Aaron whispered. "We're gonna make all of it happen, you and me."

"Sure as the sun rises, we will," she replied, her voice a soft murmur of conviction.

"Come on," Aaron said at last, releasing her with reluctance. He took her hand, his fingers lacing through hers, and pulled her toward their bedroom. He half expected her to change her mind about starting their physical relationship, and he was ready for it to happen, but he'd been ready to make love with her since the night they'd met.

After closing the door to their room, he took her into his arms and kissed her passionately, his hand stroking down her back over her bottom.

"Feels good," Deborah said softly.

"Best feeling in the world," Aaron agreed, giving her bottom a gentle squeeze.

Their embrace deepened, fueled by the unspoken promises and shared dreams that bound them together. Deborah felt a surge of desire mingled with a profound sense of security in Aaron's arms. The air was heavy with the sweet scent of wildflowers, carried inside by the gentle breeze that rustled the curtains.

Passion flared between them as they undressed each other with a tender urgency. Deborah's heart raced in anticipation, her body humming with longing.

Aaron's hands traced every curve of her body, worshipping each inch as if committing her form to memory.

Their lovemaking was a dance of whispers and sighs, an unspoken language of desire and tenderness. Deborah felt herself drowning in the depths of Aaron's gaze, lost in a world where only they existed.

THE FOLLOWING EVENING, Deborah's fingers danced over the yarn, looping and twisting with a grace born of years spent at this very task. Each stitch carried her further into a reverie of the days to come on their stretch of Texan land. She sat in a rocking chair that Aaron had made for her, its gentle motion in sync with the rhythm of her needles.

"Look at you, all lost in thought," Aaron's voice rumbled, a smile evident in his tone as he leaned against the porch post, watching her.

"Just thinking about tomorrow... and all the tomorrows after that," she replied without looking up, her blue eyes focused on the growing fabric in her lap.

"Good thoughts, I hope," he said, stepping over to sit beside her on the porch steps.

"Only the best," Deborah assured him, finally glancing up to meet his gaze. "Dreams of little feet running across these boards, laughter filling the air."

"Sounds perfect," Aaron mused.

As twilight deepened, the first stars began to blink into existence above them, competing with the soft glow emanating from the windows of their home. Deborah set aside her knitting, the half-finished sock forgotten for the moment, and joined Aaron on the steps.

"Beautiful, isn't it?" she whispered.

"Nothing more beautiful than this," Aaron agreed, his arm finding its way around her shoulders. Together, they watched the night sky put on its show, each star a beacon of the life they were destined to share.

"Promise me we'll always take a moment to watch the stars," Deborah said.

"Every night, if you want," came his earnest reply.

And in that moment, Deborah knew that life with Aaron was everything she'd ever dreamed of.

Chapter Nine

Deborah sat on the porch of her home. Aaron Tudor stood toe-to-toe with Thomas Kinkirk, an outsider whose reputation for trouble was as widespread as the prairie.

"You've got no right to fence off what isn't yours, Kinkirk!" Aaron's voice boomed across the expanse, his tone betraying the ire he seldom showed.

"Your land? Ha! That's a laugh, Tudor," scoffed Kinkirk, his thin lips twisting into a sneer. "I'll run my cattle wherever I please."

Deborah's hand faltered, the half-finished sock dangling from her needles. Her heart thudded, each beat echoing the intensity of the men's stares. She knew Aaron to be kind and fair. The man, who Deborah had briefly met, must truly be doing something wrong to get Aaron so upset.

Kinkirk jabbed a finger towards Aaron's broad chest, the aggression clear even from the distance. Deborah's breath caught. Aaron could handle himself in a fight—she had no doubt—but the alarming possibility of violence shook her to the core.

"Enough talk," Aaron warned, his stance unyielding as the oaks that dotted their land. "Move your herd by morning, or I'll do it for you."

A silent plea rose within Deborah, a hope that words would suffice, that the heated exchange wouldn't escalate beyond threats. She watched, her fingers knotted in the yarn, as Aaron and Kinkirk locked eyes, neither willing to back down. The tension hung in the air, thick as molasses, and in that moment, all of Deborah's fears seemed to converge upon the dusty ground where the two men faced off.

"Think carefully, Tudor. This ain't over," Kinkirk spat before turning on his heel and stalking away.

Aaron stood firm, watching until the outsider disappeared from view. Deborah let out the breath she hadn't realized she'd been holding. For now, the crisis was averted, but the seeds of conflict had been sown, and she knew that the peaceful life they cherished was under threat.

From her vantage point on the porch, the fading light painted the scene in hues of oranges and purples—a beautiful end to a fraught day. Deborah gathered her knitting. As night began to fall, her thoughts lingered on Aaron. She didn't know if she could handle him being in danger.

Deborah clutched the yarn in her hands, heart racing as she watched Aaron's retreat. The fading echoes of the argument with Thomas Kinkirk left a bitter taste in the air. She could intervene, demand an explanation, or perhaps even mediate. But her fingers trembled at the thought, and her fear of confrontation with any man, let alone one as volatile as Kinkirk, rooted her to the spot.

EARLY THE NEXT MORNING, there was a line of men on their land, fortifying the very fence Aaron had demanded come down.

"Deborah, you must be brave," she whispered to herself, the words a feeble attempt to stir courage within her. It wasn't just land. It was their life, their future. And right now, that future hung by a thread.

Aaron and his men formed a line on this side of the fence, and Deborah's hands shook as she wondered what she should do.

She released the yarn she'd been using to calm her nerves, letting it tumble to the wooden boards of the porch with a soft thud. Time was slipping away, and indecision was a luxury they couldn't afford. With a shaky breath, she straightened her spine—a motion uncharacteristic of her usual timid stance—and made up her mind.

"Tim and the others...they'll know what to do," she said aloud, trying to convince herself as much as the evening air.

Without allowing herself another moment to hesitate, Deborah hitched up her skirts just enough to move quickly and darted down the porch steps. She ran as fast as she could to the Stockwell ranch, knowing that Tim, Amy's husband, would help.

"Tim!" Deborah called out as she approached the neighboring property where Tim Stockwell lived, her voice stronger than she felt. The tall, no-nonsense man appeared from behind the stable door, his face creased with concern at the sight of her distress.

"Something's wrong," she managed to say between breaths.

"Slow down, Deb," Tim urged, a hint of his slow Texas drawl soothing her frayed nerves. "Tell me what happened."

"Outsiders," she replied succinctly, knowing that Tim would understand the gravity of the word in their close-knit community. "Aaron's in trouble."

"Say no more," Tim said, determination steeling his features. "I'll get Andy and the boys."

"Thank you," she breathed, relief washing over her for the first time since the argument. Together, they would stand a chance against the looming threat.

"Hurry back. We'll be there as quick as we can," Tim said, and Deborah nodded, her spirit bolstered by the prospect of their united front. They would protect their home, come what may, with the help of friends who were as steadfast as the land they cherished.

Deborah's skirts billowed around her as she sprinted across the land that stretched between Tim's property and her own. The fabric clung to her sweat-dampened skin, but there was no time for discomfort. Each stride propelled her closer to home, to Aaron, to the hope of rallying a defense against a threat that could tear apart their peaceful existence.

"Must get home," she muttered to herself, quickening her pace. Her heart hammered against her ribs like a drumbeat, urging her on despite the heat that pressed down on her with the force of an unseen hand.

When Deborah finally skidded to a halt at the ranch, her breath came in ragged gasps, yet her resolve never wavered. She grabbed the rifle Aaron had taught her to shoot just as Tim rode up with several of her brothers-in-law and David Dailey.

"Thank you," Deborah said, her voice soft but laced with gratitude. In that moment, she knew that together they were stronger than any fear that sought to divide them.

"Grab your rifles," Andrew instructed, and the men dispersed momentarily before returning armed and ready.

"Deborah, you stay put," David said. "It's gonna get messy out there."

"No," she shook her head, defiance sparking in her blue eyes. "This is my home too."

"Then let's ride out together," Joel declared, tipping his hat back with a grin.

They gathered their horses, the animals sensing the tension and snorting restlessly. With quick, practiced movements, they mounted up, forming a line of solidarity that would not easily be broken.

"All right," Tim said, appearing beside Deborah with a reassuring nod. "Let's show them what we're made of." He handed Deborah the reins of a second gelding he'd brought for her.

She mounted, riding astride, which was strange. She'd never seen a woman ride astride in Massachusetts, but she'd never seen a woman ride side saddle in Texas.

"Let's go save Aaron," Deborah said, her voice now steady with conviction. And with that, they rode out as one. They would defend their friend with everything they had.

Dust billowed beneath the thundering hooves as Deborah and her band of friends charged towards the outskirts of the ranch. Each one sat tall in the saddle, faces set like flint, eyes fixed on the horizon where their friend and neighbor, Aaron Tudor, stood his ground.

"Keep close," Tim called out over the din, his voice a beacon of steadiness in the turmoil.

"Right behind you!" Andrew's shout followed, the glint of the afternoon sun reflecting off the rifle cradled in his arm.

The ranch hands huddled around Aaron, forming a rugged barrier against Thomas Kinkirk and his gang. But the odds were even at best – for each man loyal to the ranch, there stood an outsider with a scowl and a loaded gun.

"Stay strong, boys!" Aaron's deep voice boomed across the divide, barely audible over the cacophony of curses and the cocking of weapons.

"Ready up, we're almost there!" Joel's eyes gleamed with a fierce light as he spurred his horse to greater speeds.

They arrived just as the first shot cracked through the stifling heat, a violent crescendo that set the tone for the ensuing chaos. Gunfire erupted from both sides. Shouts and yells tore through the air, a wild symphony accompanying the dance of death that unfolded before them.

"Take cover!" David yelled, ducking low as a bullet whizzed past him.

"Circle around, flank them!" Tim directed, steering his mount expertly as they sought to gain the advantage.

Deborah's heart raced, the rhythm matching the relentless beat of hooves on the hard ground. She clutched Tim's shoulders tightly, resolved not to let her fear dictate her actions. They had come to fight, to protect what was theirs, and she would stand by Aaron, come hell or high water.

"Push them back!" Aaron roared, his presence commanding even amidst the chaos.

"Stay strong, Deborah!" Joel encouraged, noticing the flicker of uncertainty in her eyes.

"Can't let them win," she muttered to herself, steeling her nerves.

The battle raged on, a bitter struggle under the unforgiving Texas sun, but inch by inch, Aaron and his friends fought bravely. The outsiders, met with unexpected resistance, began faltering in their assault, their numbers no longer an assurance of victory.

"Y'all aren't taking this land!" Andy bellowed, his defiance punctuated by the crack of his rifle.

With every passing moment, the tide turned ever so slightly in favor of the defenders, their unity and resolve proving stronger than the invaders' brute force. And through it all, Deborah's thoughts remained steadfast on Aaron's safety and the future they were fighting for, side by side.

Deborah's eyes scanned the chaos as she loaded her rifle with practiced hands. She said a silent prayer of thanks that Aaron had taught her to shoot. Dust and gunpowder stung the air, and the sounds of battle hung heavy over the land she'd come to call home. She took a deep breath, letting the familiar motion of sliding the bullet into place calm her shaking fingers.

"Watch out, Deborah!" David's voice cut through the din, his warning sharp but not unkind.

She ducked instinctively, a bullet whizzing past where her head had been moments before. A tight smile tugged at her lips—her reflexes were quicker than she'd given herself credit for.

"Thanks!" she called back, her voice surprisingly steady.

Aaron was nearby, a giant among men, his rifle roaring like thunder. Each time he fired, an invader fell, yet still they pressed on. Deborah's heart lurched with every shot that came too close to him, and she felt an urgent need to act—to do something more.

"Cover me," she said to Joel, who nodded, understanding the unspoken plan in her determined gaze.

"Be careful," he replied, his words almost lost in the cacophony.

With a quick nod, she urged her horse forward, maneuvering closer to Aaron. Her eyes never left him, tracking each movement as if tied by an invisible string. The bond they shared wasn't just one of land and livelihood—it was something deeper, born of quiet moments and mutual respect.

"Deborah, get back!" Aaron's voice boomed, a mix of concern and command.

"Not a chance," she muttered, lifting her rifle and taking aim.

Her finger tightened around the trigger, and the rifle kicked against her shoulder. One of the outsiders threatening Aaron's flank crumpled to the ground. Relief flooded her for a brief moment before another wave of adversaries surged forward.

"Nice shot!" Tim hollered from somewhere to her right, his own gunfire punctuating his praise.

"Focus. Protect." These two words became her mantra, a lifeline amidst the whirlwind of violence.

Aaron's eyes met hers across the battlefield, a silent thank you conveyed in their depths. But there was no time to acknowledge it. They were fighting for their future, every bullet and every breath counting towards victory or defeat.

"Stay safe, Aaron," she whispered, knowing he might not hear her over the roar of conflict but needing to say it all the same.

"Always," he mouthed back, before turning to face the next threat.

Deborah's heart pounded, her knuckles white on the reins and rifle. But within her, a newfound courage simmered, ready to face whatever this land and love asked of her.

Sweat dripped from Deborah's brow, mixing with the dirt and gunpowder that clung to her skin. She loaded another round into her rifle with practiced ease, her movements a stark contrast to the trembling fear that had once gripped her at the mere thought of conflict. Now, there was no room for fear.

"Deb, now!" Andrew Forsythe's voice cut through the din, signaling the moment they had been waiting for.

She nodded, heart racing, and peered through the haze. The outsiders, once an indomitable force, showed the first signs of faltering under the relentless defense of Aaron and his ragtag band of ranch hands and neighbors. Deborah's fingers tightened around the rifle as she took aim once more, her breath a silent count before the shot rang out.

"Keep pushing!" Joel Trinity shouted, his hat flying off as he spurred his horse forward, leading a charge that seemed to breathe new life into their ranks.

Aaron, amidst the fray, fought with the strength of ten men, his dark hair clinging to his forehead as he swung with precision and power. His presence alone seemed to embolden their side, rallying them as though he were not just a man, but the very spirit of the land they called home.

"Fall back!" The cry came from one of the outsiders, the panic in his voice spreading like wildfire through their numbers.

And just like that, the tide turned. Deborah watched, almost in disbelief, as the group of menacing strangers began to retreat, scrambling away from the ranch they had so boldly sought to claim. The sound of gunfire dwindled, replaced by the thundering hooves of the fleeing trespassers.

"Yee-haw!" David Dailey couldn't contain his jubilation, his whoop joining the collective sigh of relief that swept over them.

"Deborah, you did good," Tim Stockwell said, tipping his hat to her with a weary smile.

"Thanks, Tim." Her voice was a soft murmur, almost lost in the vastness of the open prairie.

Looking around, she saw the exhaustion mirrored on the faces of her friends, yet each of them wore a grin of victory. They had stood together, shoulder to shoulder, and defended not just a piece of earth, but a shared dream of peace and prosperity.

"Let's get back to the ranch," Aaron suggested, his voice gentle but carrying the weight of authority. "We've got work to do."

"Right behind you," Deborah replied, her blue eyes meeting his brown ones with unspoken gratitude. They had weathered the storm, their bond unbroken and stronger than ever.

"Home," she whispered to herself, the word a sweet promise as they turned their horses toward the setting sun, leaving the field of battle behind.

Deborah dismounted with care, her legs unsteady as if she had been riding for days without rest. Around her, the others gathered, their silhouettes etched against the dimming light of the Texan sky. Joel was already checking on David's arm, which hung awkwardly at his side.

"Let me see that," Deborah said, moving closer to inspect David's injury.

"Ah, it's nothing," David muttered, trying to wave her off with his good hand. But Deborah wasn't having any of that.

"Sit down before you fall down," she insisted. With a sheepish grin, David complied.

"Looks like you'll live," she announced after a careful examination, tying a makeshift bandage with the efficiency only a knitter could muster.

"Thanks, Deb," David replied, his smile genuine despite the pain.

"Anybody else need patching up?" Deborah asked, looking around at the faces of her friends.

"Andrew caught a bullet graze, but he's too stubborn to admit it hurts," Tim chimed in, clapping Andrew on the back with a chuckle.

"Could've been worse," Andrew grunted, his eyes meeting Deborah's with quiet thanks.

"Good thing we're all too tough for our own good," Joel added, and a round of laughter softened the harsh memory of the day.

"Where's Aaron?" Deborah suddenly realized she hadn't seen him since the last shot was fired.

"Right here," came a reply from behind her. Deborah spun around to find Aaron stepping towards them, his face smeared with dirt, but his eyes bright with relief.

"Thank goodness," she breathed out, rushing to his side. Her hands hovered over him, searching for injuries, but finding none, she simply allowed herself to be pulled into a reassuring embrace.

"Couldn't let anything happen to me," Aaron mused, his voice low. "Who'd help you herd these cats?"

"Suppose you're right," Deborah said, pulling back just enough to look up at him with a playful glint in her eyes. "But don't think this means you can start slacking."

"Wouldn't dream of it," Aaron promised, his smile broadening.

After all the others had left, Deborah turned to Aaron. "Quite a day, huh?" she said, her voice steady despite the turmoil that had churned within her only hours before.

"Yep, quite a day," Aaron agreed, his deep voice rumbling softly. His gaze held hers, warm and unwavering, as if nothing could break the connection between them now. "And it's not even noon yet."

Deborah leaned into him, resting her head against his broad chest. The steady beat of his heart was a comfort, a reminder of life's simple continuance after such chaos. "I was scared," she confessed, though it wasn't like her to admit such things.

"Me too," Aaron admitted, wrapping his arm around her shoulders. "But knowing you were out there, fighting alongside us... It made all the difference."

"Tomorrow's gonna be another scorcher," Deborah said, finally breaking the calm. She smiled, thinking of the heat, the work awaiting them, and the relentless Texas sun. "More fences to mend, I think."

"Seems there's always something," Aaron replied with a chuckle. His thumb brushed gently over her knuckles, a silent vow of solidarity. "But we'll handle it."

"Always together," Deborah affirmed, feeling the truth of those words deep in her bones.

Chapter Ten

The air was still over the ranch, a deceptive calm before the storm. Deborah stood on the porch of Brenda's house, her gaze stretching out to the horizon where a thin ribbon of smoke curled skyward. A sudden barrage of gunfire splintered the silence, sending a flock of birds into frenzied flight. She flinched at the sound, her heart pounding a rapid staccato against her ribs.

"Lord have mercy," she whispered, blue eyes wide as the distant echo of chaos breached the quiet of her afternoon.

"Deborah!" Aaron's voice cut through the tension. "Get inside, now!"

She nodded, her hands trembling as she clutched the knitting needles she had somehow forgotten to put down. The sound of another gunshot made her jump, and the ball of yarn tumbled from her grasp, rolling across the wooden planks.

"Keep your head down," Aaron instructed, ushering her toward safety. His deep voice was steady, a comforting rumble amid the chaos.

"Are they coming closer?" Deborah's voice barely rose above a whisper, her fear rendering her usual soft-spoken tone even quieter.

"Can't tell yet." Aaron's eyes scanned the horizon, his protective instincts as evident as the concern etched on his brow. "We'll be ready for them either way."

"Ready?" Deborah asked, a flicker of incredulity on her face. "How does one get ready for such madness?"

"By sticking together," Aaron said simply, a hand resting briefly on her shoulder in a gesture meant to reassure. "We're not alone in this, Deborah."

She managed a small nod, taking a shaky breath as she watched the smoke thicken in the distance. In that moment, she wished for nothing more than the soothing rhythm of her knitting, a small comfort against the backdrop of an escalating range war.

"Come on," he urged gently. "Let's see what we can do to shore up the defenses." Already there were ranch hands on duty watching for an escalation of the violence at all times. There was a signal for the neighbors who had promised to help. Three shots, and they would all come. And those who were further out would echo the shots, so it could be heard further away.

"All right," she agreed. Together, they stepped back into the house, the sound of their boots against the floorboards resolute in the face of uncertainty.

Deborah stepped into Brenda's parlor, a haven of camaraderie amid the turmoil outside. The room was filled with her sisters and friends, all gathered around a quilt that sprawled across their laps as they stitched in unison. Worried faces turned toward her as she entered.

"Deborah, come sit," Brenda beckoned, patting a cushion next to her. "We're just talking about what's been happening."

"Thank you," Deborah replied. Her hands fidgeted in her lap, missing the familiar needles and yarn that often calmed her.

"Can't make heads or tails of this senseless fighting," said Ruth, shaking her head, her fingers never pausing in their work. "But we've got each other, and that counts for something." Ruth was a member of their congregation, and someone they all adored.

"Sure does," Susan said, offering Deborah a smile. "And we've got your back, honey."

Deborah looked at the circle of determined faces, feeling the weight of her worries lighten ever so slightly. "I'm just scared is all," she admitted. "For Aaron, for the ranch... for us."

"Of course, you are," Brenda said, her tone soothing as she laid a comforting hand over Deborah's. "But remember, you're stronger than you think. You've built a life here, and you'll defend it."

"Stronger together," Ruth added with a nod.

"You're right," Deborah said, drawing strength from their reassurance. "We can get through this."

"Exactly," Brenda agreed, her eyes sparkling with encouragement. "Now, let's get to stitching and planning."

"Deborah, I won't lie to you," Cassandra said, her voice barely above a whisper, "I hear those gunshots, and my heart speeds up every time. Feels like the whole world's on a knifepoint."

"Mine too," Jane agreed, tucking a loose strand of hair behind her ear. "But then I remember we're not alone in this. We're a family."

"That we are," Deborah responded, feeling the tremor in her own voice. She glanced around, the faces of her sisters and friends etched with worry yet lined with determination.

"Family doesn't let family face troubles single-handed," Brenda said, her eyes meeting each of theirs in turn.

"Very true," acknowledged Ruth, her hands now still. "And families stick together when the wind blows fierce."

"Then let's think about what we can do," Deborah proposed, the seed of an idea beginning to sprout. "We've got smarts and numbers. We just need a plan."

"We need to build barriers first," Amy suggested, her brow furrowed in thought. "We could stack those hay bales high by the fences."

"Good thinking," Susan nodded. "And those thorny bushes too. Make it tough for any unwanted guests."

"Aaron's got that Winchester rifle," Brenda mused. "He's a good shot, but he can't be everywhere at once. Maybe we start practicing some shooting ourselves."

"Shooting? Us?" Cassandra chuckled nervously.

"Never too late to learn," Deborah stated firmly. "Aaron taught me to shoot shortly after we got here."

"Deborah's right," Imogene confirmed. "We'll stand by Aaron and our homes."

"Let's hope it doesn't come to that," Hannah sighed, "but better ready than sorry."

"Tomorrow, we start," Deborah announced.

DEBORAH'S HEART WAS a wild thing in her chest, thrumming with fear and determination as she watched the horizon, where plumes of smoke rose like specters against the late afternoon sky. She swallowed hard, the taste of dust and anxiety thick on her tongue.

"Come away from there," a gentle voice called from behind her. It was Susan. "You're borrowing trouble and letting worry eat at you."

Deborah turned, feeling the weight of her fears lessen just a smidgen at the sight of Susan's calm demeanor. "Susan, I... How do you do it? Stand so strong when the world's trying to knock you down?"

Susan chuckled softly, pulling Deborah into the cool shade of the porch. "Strength isn't about never being scared. It's about what you do when fear comes around. You're stronger than you think, Deborah Tudor."

"Feels like I'm just playing at bravery," Deborah confessed, her fingers twisting the fabric of her apron.

"Playing or not, it's there inside you," Susan assured her, reaching out to still Deborah's restless hands with her own. "You've got a light in you that this range war can't snuff out. Remember that."

"Thank you, Susan," Deborah said.

"Go on now, get to your knitting. I've seen how those needles and yarn work better than anything else for your nerves," Susan said, giving Deborah a knowing smile.

"Guess it couldn't hurt," Deborah replied, mustering a small smile of her own as she retrieved her knitting basket.

She settled into a wicker chair, the creak of its weave familiar and soothing. With each click and slide of her needles, Deborah felt the tight coil of fear inside her begin to unwind. Yarn over, through, pull, and off. The emerging pattern of the sock was simple, nothing fancy, but each stitch made her feel just a little bit better.

DEBORAH TUCKED HER latest knitted creation into the basket and stood up, smoothing out the folds of her cotton dress. The evening breeze carried a hint of jasmine and the distant murmur of voices. She walked down the porch steps, her sisters Gail and Hannah right behind her. It was time to weave the community as tightly as the patterns in her knitting.

"Deborah, do you think people will help?" Hannah asked, her voice tinged with hope.

"Only one way to find out," Deborah replied, squaring her shoulders. They made their way along the dusty path toward the neighboring farm.

At the first house, a gray-wooden structure with shutters hanging askew, they were greeted by Mrs. Mueller, whose apron was as worn as the smile lines around her eyes.

"Girls, what brings y'all this way?" Mrs. Mueller inquired, wiping her hands on her apron.

"Mrs. Mueller, we need to talk about the range war. It's getting closer, and Aaron could use some help," Deborah explained, her voice steady despite the flutter in her chest.

"Say no more," Mrs. Mueller said, nodding decisively. "We'll gather the men. Your husband won't stand alone."

"Thank you kindly," Gail said, her relief evident.

"Let's spread the word," Deborah suggested, feeling a surge of gratitude.

They continued from house to house, receiving nods, firm handshakes, and promises of support. By nightfall, they had rallied a small but determined group, ready to stand together against the encroaching threat.

BACK AT BRENDA'S HOUSE, Deborah sat under the stars, the warm night air brushing against her skin. She thought of the day's efforts, of the faces that had shown concern and the hands that had been extended in friendship.

She had faced her fears head-on, learned to reach out, and found a community willing to reach back. Yes, she still trembled at the sound of gunfire, and yes, she still hesitated when speaking to men. But she was no longer the same woman who hid behind her knitting, hoping problems would pass her by.

"Look at you, all thoughtful under the moonlight," Gail teased, joining her on the grass.

"Was just thinking how much I've changed," Deborah admitted.

"Change is good," Hannah said, sitting on Deborah's other side. "Shows you're alive."

A distant crack shattered the stillness. Deborah's heart skipped a beat, and she clutched at the grass beneath her fingers, feeling the prick of the blades.

"Did you hear that?" Hannah whispered, her voice tight with worry.

"Sounds like trouble brewing again," Gail said, standing abruptly, eyes scanning the horizon where darkness met the faint glow of the homestead lights.

"Could be hunters," Deborah said hopefully. But another volley of gunfire, closer this time, cut through her denial.

"Too late for hunting," Hannah said, rising to her feet beside Gail.

The three sisters stood huddled together. A plume of smoke began to rise from the direction of their neighbors' property, twisting into the night sky like a dark omen.

"Lord almighty," Deborah murmured, her earlier resolve hardening into a steely determination.

"Deborah, what do we do?" Hannah asked.

"We stand by each other," Deborah replied firmly. "We've faced storms before."

"Let's get inside," Gail urged, "We need to warn Aaron."

They moved as one, swift and silent across the dew-kissed grass. Inside, the warm glow of lamplight seemed a world away from the chaos outside.

"Should we light the lanterns on the porch? Signal to the others?" Hannah questioned.

"Could draw fire," Gail said. "We should shoot three times, like we've arranged."

"I agree with Gail," Deborah said, her voice steady even as her hands betrayed her with a slight tremble.

"All right," Gail said, picking up her rifle.

"God protect us," Deborah said. "God and a good Winchester," Deborah added, retrieving another rifle from its place above the mantel.

"Never thought I'd see you holding one of those," Hannah commented, a hint of her usual humor returning.

"Neither did I," Deborah admitted, hefting the weapon.

"Deborah, look!" Gail pointed towards a shadow moving against the backdrop of the burning field.

"Friend or foe?" Hannah asked, her hand instinctively reaching for the rifle.

"Can't tell," Deborah said, squinting into the darkness.

"Best be ready for either," Gail said, her voice carrying a note of finality.

"Always am," Deborah replied, her grip tightening on the rifle.

A figure emerged from the smoke, striding purposefully toward them.

"Stand down, it's Aaron!" Deborah recognized the confident gait of her husband.

Relief flooded through her, yet the unease lingered, a reminder that this night was far from over.

"Trouble's coming our way," Aaron called out as he neared, urgency etched in his features.

"Then we'll meet it together," Deborah answered, her voice betraying none of the fear that twisted in her gut.

"Get inside. Barricade the doors," Aaron instructed. "I'll round up the men. We make our stand tonight."

Deborah nodded.

"Be safe," Hannah said.

"Always," he replied with a quick, reassuring squeeze of Deborah's arm before turning back into the night.

"Come on," Gail urged, pulling Deborah and Hannah back inside.

As they fortified the house, the sound of galloping hooves and rallying cries grew louder. Deborah glanced out the window one last time, watching as figures mounted on horseback gathered in the distance, silhouetted against the fires that now raged unabated.

"Whatever comes," Deborah said, meeting her sisters' gazes, "we face it as family."

Outside, a shout rose above the cacophony—a battle cry that set the night ablaze with defiance and fear. Deborah clenched her jaw, steeling herself for the fight ahead, knowing that the next hours would test the very fabric of their bond.

Chapter Eleven

The world seemed to tilt on its axis as Deborah Tudor caught sight of Aaron now reduced to a crumpled form lying in the dust. Her heart, which had always beat a little faster at the sight of him, now hammered with terror. "Aaron!" she cried out, her voice breaking through the stillness.

She knelt beside him, her hands trembling as they hovered over his broad chest, afraid to touch, afraid to cause more harm. His breaths were shallow, and his once ruddy cheeks were pale, a stark contrast to the dark hair that lay matted with sweat upon his brow. To see such vitality so diminished sent a chill through Deborah, despite the summer heat.

"Stay with me, Aaron," she whispered, her soft-spoken tone laced with urgency. She brushed back a lock of his hair with tenderness.

Gathering the hem of her simple dress, she pressed it against a wound on his arm to stem the bleeding. Her mind raced—memories of her time at the foundling home, where she'd often helped bandage minor injuries of the younger children, came to the forefront. Never had she imagined applying such skills to the strongest man she knew.

"Deborah," Aaron's deep voice rumbled weakly, his brown eyes finding hers. The warmth there, even amid his pain, fueled her resolve.

"Shh, save your strength," she said.

Deborah stood, her gaze sweeping over their home—the ranch they had both poured their souls into. She took a deep breath, feeling the weight of responsibility settle onto her slight shoulders. The air tasted of dust and determination.

"Can't let them take this from us," she murmured to herself. With each heartbeat, she felt an unfamiliar firmness take root within her.

"Help's coming, Aaron," Deborah assured him, but there was no one in sight, just the endless stretch of Texas prairie. She would have to be the help. For Aaron. For their dreams of children and a life filled with more than just average days.

"Deborah," he managed again.

"Quiet now," she soothed, patting his hand. "You rest. I've got work to do."

Fixing her blue eyes on the horizon, where danger approached like a storm cloud, Deborah understood what she must do. A calmness settled over her, the kind that comes when there's no room left for doubt or fear.

"Those Kinkirk boys don't know who they're messing with," she said softly. She helped Aaron to a shady spot beneath an old oak tree, ensuring he was comfortable before rising to her feet.

"Watch over him," she instructed the ranch dog, who had been lying nearby with ears perked. The animal gave a soft woof and nuzzled Aaron's hand with a wet nose.

Deborah turned toward the house, her steps purposeful. She wouldn't let anyone harm what was theirs—not while she still drew breath. Today, she would fight not only for Aaron but also for herself—for the woman she was becoming amid adversity.

"Let's show them what we're made of," she said. It was time. Time to defend, to protect, to love.

Deborah's gaze darted across the expanse of their ranch, her mind racing as swiftly as her heart. The oppressive heat of summer shimmered above the land, but her focus remained sharp. Aaron's injury had lit a fire within her, and she would not let it be smothered by fear or hesitation.

"Land's got more secrets than a Sunday sermon," she muttered to herself, recalling the countless hours spent roaming these acres. She knew every dip and rise, each tree that offered shelter, and the rocks that could trip up an unwary foot.

With nimble steps, she made for the barn. Inside, her hands moved with practiced ease, gathering ropes and finding her rifle, which was shorter than Aaron's and easier for her to use.

"Should've been just another peaceful day," she sighed, eyeing the collection, "but I think peace has to be fought for sometimes."

She strode out, surveying the terrain once more. Deborah's thoughts flew to a hidden path, one that skirted the edge of the property—a narrow trail overgrown with brush, easy to miss if you didn't know it was there. It snaked behind a thicket of mesquite trees, offering a covered approach to the backside of the house where she could surprise anyone who dared threaten their home.

"All right, this is it," she whispered to herself. She took a moment, letting the stillness of the land seep into her bones. Then, like a shadow, she slipped onto the path, the rifle slung over one shoulder.

As she moved, her feet found the familiar grooves of the earth, her body remembering the way even as her mind stayed alert. The path twisted and turned, and she followed it, using the natural cover to her advantage. Each step took her closer to where she would make her stand.

"Deborah Tudor," she said, a smile flickering across her lips despite the tension that thrummed through her veins, "defender of hearth and home."

Her blue eyes sparkled with a hint of mischief, a lightness in her spirit. There was something empowering about standing on the soil that fed and nurtured them, about knowing she would do whatever it took to protect it.

"Let's hope they're as clumsy as they are cruel," she murmured, thinking of the intruders and their impending encounter. She positioned herself behind the thick curtain of greenery, carefully loading the rifle.

Deborah peeked through the brush, her heart hammering against her ribs. A group of men materialized from the shimmering heat. At their lead was Thomas Kinkirk, his lips curled into a sneer that promised trouble.

"Looks like we found our little mouse," Kinkirk called out, his voice carrying a taunting edge that set Deborah's nerves on edge.

Deborah crouched lower, lifting the rifle and holding it steady. She watched as they spread out, angling toward her house with a confidence that rankled. It was clear. They believed this land and everything on it was theirs for the taking.

As they drew nearer, Deborah's mind raced. Her eyes darted to the left where the old well sat, half-hidden by overgrown weeds – an obstacle that could trip up the unwary. To the right, the ground sloped away sharply, a deceptive drop that could easily twist an ankle.

"Come out, come out," one of the men jeered, his eyes scanning the terrain. "We ain't gonna hurt ya... much."

"Shh," she whispered to herself, her breaths shallow and quick.

As Kinkirk's boot crunched perilously close to her hiding spot, Deborah fired. With the element of surprise on her side, she shot right through his shoulder, just above his heart, aiming not to kill but to make it impossible for him to continue, and to scatter the men like cattle before a storm.

"Yaah!" she cried out, her voice ringing clear and defiant.

Kinkirk stumbled back, shock flashing across his face as the bullet struck just where she'd aimed. Taking advantage of their momentary confusion, Deborah pivoted, shooting next at the man who she was certain was his second in command.

"Careful now, Tommy," she taunted with a flicker of a grin, feeling a strange exhilaration. "This mouse has claws."

"Get her!" Kinkirk bellowed, his hand covering his shoulder, blood oozing out around it. But Deborah was already moving, darting away, her knowledge of the land guiding her steps as she led them on a wild chase, ducking low branches and leaping over snake holes.

She glanced back just long enough to see the men scrambling to follow, their coordination thrown off by the unfamiliar terrain. Their curses filled the air, but Deborah didn't falter. This was her home, her sanctuary, and she would defend it with every ounce of her being.

"Come on then!" she called back, her challenge ringing out across the open fields. "Let's see what you've got!"

She ran straight to the barn and up the ladder to the hay mow, where she could see the approaching men through the window. She'd made good time while the men had struggled to follow her.

She had no intention of killing anyone, but shooting them would be her pleasure. They each deserved one of her bullets because she didn't know which one of them had shot Aaron, and she would avenge her wounded husband.

Despite the fear that gnawed at her insides, adrenaline surged through her veins, lending strength to her muscles and sharpness to her senses.

"Enough of this foolishness, girl!" Alfred Kinkirk shouted as he advanced, his face twisted into a snarl.

"Your kind isn't welcome here, Kinkirk," she yelled back, taking careful aim and shooting his leg out from under him. She said a silent prayer of thanks that Aaron had the foresight to teach her to shoot as she reloaded.

Despite their leaders being down, the men continued to advance, but she was no longer afraid. She picked them off one by one, watching them fall.

Deborah stood her ground, her knuckles white around the rifle. They had hurt her husband and were coming for her home. She wouldn't be defeated.

"Come on, then!" she dared, her voice clear and steady despite the chaos.

"Yer gonna regret this," one of the men yelled at her, baring his teeth like a cornered animal.

"Maybe," she conceded with a flicker of that same defiant grin, "but not today."

With a swift movement, she shot again, forcing the man to stumble back as she shot his arm. He let out a string of expletives, threatening her.

"Better men than you have tried," she said, her heart pounding a fierce rhythm.

The standoff seemed to stretch into eternity, the summer heat pressing down upon them as a silent witness to their resolve.

"Let's end this," she whispered to herself, ready for whatever came next.

Deborah's breath came in ragged gasps, her body aching. Sweat trickled down her brow, stinging the scrapes that lined her cheek—a memento from her run through the brush. Her dress clung to her skin, the fabric torn in places, revealing bruises like storm clouds on her arms. But her grip on the rifle never wavered, her knuckles white as bone.

"Come on, Deb," she muttered to herself, "for Aaron."

Her heart clenched at the thought of him lying on the ground, his usual robust frame now frail and quiet. She blinked back hot tears, refusing to let them fall. The outsiders had brought this fight to her doorstep, threatening the life she and Aaron had built.

"Yer lookin' tired, Missy," the last man sneered, raising his own rifle. "Ready to give up yet?"

"Never," Deborah shot back, her voice stronger than she felt.

Just when her limbs threatened to give out, a new sound pierced the tense air—the thundering of hooves and the rallying cries of men. Deborah's eyes flickered past Kinkirk's shoulder, and her spirit soared. Racing toward the barn on horseback were familiar men—her brothers and neighbors, their expressions grim with resolve.

"Thought you could handle them alone, sis?" Tim called out with a grin as he swung down from his horse.

"Got a little lost on the way," David yelled, tipping his hat.

"Looks like we're just in time," said a third, the group forming a solid line in front of the barn door, which was the only way to get to Deborah.

With the support of her kin and community bolstering her courage, Deborah straightened. She met the last man's gaze once more, feeling the shift in the air. They were no longer alone, outnumbered and outgunned. They were backed by the very people who made their lives here worth fighting for.

"Seems you've got company," Deborah called down to the man, her voice steady.

"Looks like the odds aren't in your favor any longer," Adam added, cracking his knuckles.

Even their pastor, her sister Hannah's husband, was there. "On your knees!" he shouted to the last of the outsiders.

The outsider hesitated, glancing around as he took in the sight of the assembled defenders. All of his comrades on the ground around him. Deborah could feel the tide turning, the balance shifting as her loved ones stood ready to protect one of their own.

He looked at the pastor, and slowly dropped to his knees, his hands in the air. He knew he was beaten.

The air crackled with tension, the summer heat doing nothing to quell the fire that burned in each person's gaze.

"Law's here!"

Everyone froze, turning toward the new arrival. The sheriff, badge gleaming in the sunlight, sat atop his horse, a posse at his back.

"Alfred Kinkirk, you and your men are under arrest," the sheriff announced, his voice booming across the field.

A collective breath seemed to be released as the outsiders weighed their options, clearly outnumbered and now outmaneuvered by the law itself.

"Looks like we got here just in time," the sheriff said, tipping his hat at Deborah who was still in the hay mow.

"Seems so," Deborah replied, her chest heaving with the adrenaline of the moment. "I'm coming down."

"Is this the end of your troubles, Miss Deborah?" the sheriff asked, eyeing the bruised and battered woman before him.

"I sure hope so," she said with a cautious smile.

Chapter Twelve

The clank of handcuffs and the low murmur of the sheriff's orders filtered through the air as Deborah rushed down the barn ladder, her skirts grasping at each stride. Her heart thrummed with urgency. "Tim! Amos! It's Aaron—he's hurt bad."

Tim looked up from where he stood, his hat shading eyes that had seen too much sorrow. "Lead the way, Deborah," he said, his voice steady despite the worry that creased his brow.

"Where is he?" Amos asked, adjusting his hat with a practiced tilt.

"Out by the north pasture," she replied, breathless.

Without another word, the men spurred their horses into action. Tim's mount moved with purpose while Amos kept pace, riding alongside Deborah, who directed them with quick, sure gestures.

"David's gone for the doc," Tim called over to Deborah, squinting against the sun.

"Good thinking," Deborah acknowledged, trying to keep the tremble from her voice.

"Look there!" Amos pointed ahead, where a huddled shape lay near the fence line.

"Lord have mercy," whispered Tim under his breath as they dismounted.

Deborah's hands were already reaching out, her fingers gentle yet efficient as she assessed Aaron's condition. His face was etched in pain, yet the sight of friends brought a grimace that resembled a smile.

"Hey, big guy," Tim greeted Aaron, his usual stoicism giving way to concern. "We're gonna get you fixed up."

"Much obliged," Aaron managed, his voice rough like gravel on the ranch road.

"Let's get him home," Amos said.

Together, they lifted Aaron with care, mindful of his pained groans, and settled him onto Tim's horse. Deborah mounted behind him, wrapping an arm around Aaron to steady him.

"Keep your head high, Aaron. You're tougher than old boots," she murmured, her words intended to comfort even as her own heart raced with fear.

"Always am, Deb," Aaron replied, though his voice was faint.

"Let's ride," said Tim, and the group turned back toward the house.

THE SMELL OF SMOKE clung to the air as men hustled back and forth, carrying buckets of water from the trough. They doused the flames with swift, determined motions, their faces set in grim lines yet edged with the relief that the worst had passed. The fires, which had moments ago threatened to consume everything in their path, sputtered and died under the steady assault.

"Keep at it, boys," called out one of the ranch hands, his voice a rallying cry in the midst of the chaos. "These flames ain't got nothin' on us!"

Meanwhile, Tim's horse trotted up to the homestead, the journey back seeming much longer than the one out to Aaron. With every step, Deborah held tightly to Aaron, whispering words of encouragement that were for her benefit as much as his. Amos rode alongside, scanning the horizon as if his gaze could hasten the doctor's arrival.

"Easy now," Tim soothed as they brought Aaron down and into the house. The coolness of the indoors was a stark contrast to the blazing heat outside.

In the kitchen, Deborah found a basin and filled it with water, her movements practiced and sure. She fetched a cloth and turned toward

Aaron, who was propped up in a chair, his rugged face tightened in pain.

"Let me see that wound," she said gently, rolling up her sleeves.

"Deb, you don't have to—" Aaron began but cut off with a wince as Deborah cut away the arm of his shirt and carefully cleaned away the dirt and blood.

"Quiet now, Aaron. You've done enough talking," Deborah chided softly, her touch light as she worked.

"Looks like we owe you again, Deborah," Amos remarked, standing by the doorway, his eyes reflecting the gratitude they all felt.

"None of that, Amos," she replied without looking up. "We take care of our own here."

"Can't argue with that," Tim added, leaning against the doorframe. His eyes met Deborah's, and he offered her a small, reassuring smile. "I feel bad that we were fooled by the fires and gunshots. We rode toward them, leaving Aaron to stand against the outsiders on his own. And after he was injured, you had to stand alone. Men are supposed to be the ones defending their women."

Deborah shook her head. "I was trickier than they were. That's all."

"It's a good thing. We were all surprised to follow the sound of the gunfire and find you holed up in that hayloft."

"I just did what Aaron taught me to do. I shot straight and hit what I aimed at."

Tim shook his head. "I think we're all impressed with the way you handled things. Now we need the doc to patch Aaron up and all will be well."

"Let's just hope that doctor rides as fast as David claimed," Deborah said, finishing up with the wound. She covered it with a clean cloth, her fingers lingering for a moment on Aaron's arm. "You stay with us, you hear?"

"Wouldn't dream of leaving," Aaron murmured, managing a weak grin.

"Good," Deborah said, her voice firm but kind. "Because I'm not done fussing over you yet."

The doctor's buggy clattered to a halt outside Deborah's home. She stood on the porch, wringing her hands in anticipation. The door creaked open, and the doctor stepped out, his bag in hand.

"Show me to the patient," he said curtly, tipping his hat at Deborah.

"Right this way, Doctor," she replied, leading him inside.

Aaron lay still on the bed, a grimace etched across his face. The doctor knelt beside him, examining the wound with a critical eye. He shook his head slowly, tsking under his breath.

"Mrs. Tudor, I won't sugarcoat it. This is going to be a tough one. Likely to get infected, being as ugly as it is," he remarked, glancing up at her.

Deborah swallowed hard, nodding. "Just tell me what to do, Doctor."

"Keep it clean, for starters. Change the dressing twice a day, and make sure he drinks plenty of water. If fever sets in, send someone for me straight away."

"I will, Doctor. Thank you."

As the doctor packed up his things, there were loud sounds outside. Brenda burst through the door, followed by Amy, Cassandra, Erna, Faith, Gail, Hannah, Imogene, and Jane, their faces flushed from the ride over.

"Deb! We came as soon as we heard," Brenda exclaimed, her hands on her hips as she surveyed the room. "How can we help?"

Deborah sighed in relief. "I'm sure glad to see all of you. The doctor just left, and Aaron needs careful watching."

"Then careful watching he shall have," Cassandra chimed in, her voice soft but determined.

"Let's get to work, ladies," Brenda announced, rolling up her sleeves. "We've got a ranch to run and a man to mend."

"First things first," Erna interjected. "Who's making soup? Aaron's going to need his strength."

"Charlotte's working on that now," Deborah said, a small smile breaking through her worry. "That's one less thing on my mind."

"Rest easy, Deb," Brenda reassured her. "Together, there's nothing we can't handle."

"Thank you, Brenda," Deborah said, feeling the weight on her shoulders lighten ever so slightly. "It means the world to me."

"Anytime, Deb," Brenda replied with a wink. "After all, what are sisters for?"

Deborah watched as the women dispersed, their skirts swishing against the wooden floorboards. "Amy, Hannah, could you two handle the milking?" she asked, her voice surprisingly steady given the churn of worry in her stomach.

"Course we can, Deb," Amy replied with a cheerful nod, already moving toward the door with Hannah close behind.

"Imogene, Jane, gather eggs, please. And keep an eye out for any stray ones the hens might've hidden," Deborah added, her blue eyes scanning the group for volunteers.

"Got it, Deb," said Jane, tipping an imaginary hat. Imogene just smiled and followed, her quiet demeanor a steady presence.

"Erna, Faith," Deborah continued, her gaze now landing on the remaining women, "would you mind searching for the ranch hands? We need to know how they fared."

"Consider them found. We'll take the wagon," Erna said with determination, Faith giving a small, encouraging nod.

The Texas sun hung heavy in the sky as Deborah watched her friends set about their tasks. She wiped a bead of sweat from her brow and returned to Aaron's bedside. It wasn't long before the women started returning, each one bearing news or goods in hand.

"Found them, Deb," Faith reported breathlessly as she and Erna returned, dust coating their dresses. "But it's not pretty—every last one of them is hurt. We got them all in the wagon, and we're helping them inside."

"Lord have mercy," Deborah murmured, her heart sinking. "We'll need the doctor again."

"Already sent David to fetch him," Brenda assured her, patting Deborah's shoulder with a calloused hand.

The doctor arrived, his bag of instruments clinking softly with each step. He went to work, examining each injured hand with a practiced eye. The men were stoic, their faces tight with pain but trying to remain strong in front of the women.

"Several will need to go to Fort Worth," the doctor said gravely after his assessments. "I fear they may not make it if they don't get proper care."

"Then to Fort Worth they must go," Brenda stated, her voice brooking no argument. "We'll see to it. We just have to get them back into the wagon. Which ones need to go to the hospital there?"

"Thank you all," Deborah said, feeling a wellspring of gratitude for these strong women.

As the sun dipped below the horizon, casting long shadows across the ranch, the men gathered in the dimming light on the porch. Deborah stood with them, her hands folded in front of her dress, a smudge of dirt on her cheek that she hadn't noticed. The men exchanged resolute nods, their faces set with determination.

"Look here," Amos began, his voice steady as he addressed the others. "Aaron's laid up, and these lands won't tend themselves. I think we can each take a day to fill in. We can all spare a ranch hand now and then to make up for all the ones injured."

"Right," Tim chimed in, tipping his hat back with a thumb. "I'm in for Thursdays."

One by one, the men declared their chosen days, pledging their time and effort to keep the ranch running. It was decided with the quiet strength that came from years of facing trials together. Deborah listened, her heart swelling with gratitude at their kindness.

"Deborah, you just focus on Aaron," said Amos, turning to her with a reassuring smile. "We'll handle the rest."

"Thank you," she replied, her voice barely above a whisper, but each man heard the depth of her thanks.

With a plan in place, the group dispersed, leaving Deborah alone on the porch. The last traces of daylight vanished, and the night air carried a hint of relief from the heat of the day.

Inside, the house was filled with the comforting aroma of chicken broth simmering on the stove. Charlotte moved about the kitchen with practiced ease, wooden spoon in hand. She glanced over her shoulder as Deborah entered, offering a tired but warm smile.

"Broth's almost ready," Charlotte said, stirring the pot gently. "It'll help him if fever sets in."

"Let me," Deborah offered, taking the spoon. Charlotte nodded and stepped aside, watching as Deborah's gentle hands took over the task. The rhythmic motion was soothing, almost meditative, and for a moment, Deborah allowed herself to get lost in it.

They carried a steaming bowl to Aaron's bedside together. He lay there, a giant felled by injury, his breaths coming in uneven rasps. Despite his delirium, when Deborah touched his hand, he seemed to calm, the lines of pain softening around his eyes.

"Here, love," she whispered, bringing a spoonful of broth to his lips. "This will make you strong again."

Aaron managed a weak nod, sipping the liquid with a faint sigh of contentment. Deborah's gaze lingered on his face, seeing beyond the fever to the kind-hearted man who she loved with everything inside her.

The room settled into a quiet rhythm: the tick of the clock, the whisper of the wind outside, the soft clinking of the spoon. Within the walls of the ranch house, there was warmth, there was care, and most importantly, there was hope.

Chapter Thirteen

Deborah's heart hammered against her chest as she laid her palm on Aaron's forehead. It was hot to the touch. His breath came in shallow, ragged gasps, his strong frame now shivering under the thin blanket.

Deborah hurried to the door. "Adam," she called out, her voice steady despite the panic that knotted her stomach. "Fetch the doctor, quick."

Adam, who had been tending to the horses, dashed into the room, his boots thudding against the wooden floorboards. One glance at Aaron, and he needed no further urging. "On my way," he said with a nod, tipping his hat before hurrying back out into the growing light.

Deborah smoothed back Aaron's hair, murmuring words meant to comfort them both. Her hands, usually so sure when tending the garden or mending clothes, trembled slightly as she adjusted the damp cloth on his brow.

It wasn't long before the doctor arrived, his bag of instruments clinking softly as he stepped through the door. He was a man of few words but sharp eyes that missed nothing. He examined Aaron with practiced hands, lifting an eyelid, checking his pulse, looking at the wound, and then finally standing straight with a serious look on his weathered face.

"Mrs. Tudor," the doctor began, his voice as gruff as the dry Texas land, "Aaron needs to be in the hospital. This infection is beyond what home care can manage."

A protest formed on Deborah's lips. She wanted to argue, to claim she could nurse him back to health herself. But then she met the doctor's gaze, saw the unspoken gravity there, and she knew better.

"All right," she agreed, her voice barely above a whisper. "I trust you, Doctor. We'll do whatever it takes."

"Good," the doctor replied with a small nod. "I'll arrange for the transport. He's in good hands."

As the men prepared to move Aaron, Deborah stood by, her heart aching with worry. Yet, even amid the fear, she clung to a flicker of hope. Love and companionship were the cornerstones of this community, and with their support, she believed they would weather this storm too.

DEBORAH PACED THE HOSPITAL corridor, her footsteps echoing off the sterile walls. With each pass by the ward's door, she stole a glance at Aaron, lying still on the cot, his chest rising and falling with labored breaths. Days turned into weeks, yet she remained by his side.

"Ma'am, visiting hours are over," the duty nurse reminded her gently one evening, her eyes soft with understanding.

"But I can't leave him," Deborah whispered, her voice laced with desperation.

"Come now, you need your rest too," the nurse urged, guiding Deborah away from the ward.

Reluctantly, Deborah allowed herself to be led to the front entrance. She stepped out into the warm Texas night, the air heavy with the scent of wildflowers and dust. Lantern in hand, she made her way to the nearby boarding house, its windows aglow with welcoming light.

Mrs. Garvey, the boarding house owner, met her at the door. "You look all tuckered out, dear," she said, her voice a comforting drawl. "I saved you some supper if you're hungry."

"Thank you," Deborah managed, her exhaustion evident. "I'm not hungry, but I think I need to eat so I can keep visiting Aaron."

"We're all rootin' for your Aaron."

Deborah was back at Aaron's side as soon as visiting hours started. She caught snippets of conversation from the other ranch hands in the ward, their familiar banter a strange contrast to the sterile environment.

"Hey, Deb," called out Sam, one of the hands, from his cot. "Is Aaron getting any better? We're all worried about him."

"That bullet had bad manners," Deborah replied, attempting a smile. "It gave him an infection, and he's just not doing well. I have faith though."

"Bullet don't stand a chance against The Gentle Giant," chimed in another hand, Pete.

"Sure don't," agreed the third, Billy, his voice weak but spirited. "Aaron's too stubborn to let a little fever beat him."

Their words were meant to buoy her spirits, and in some small way, they did. The days blurred into one another, but the ranch hands' encouragement never waned, nor did Deborah's resolve. As she sat knitting beside Aaron's bed, her fingers worked the yarn into patterns of hope and strength, a tangible representation of the community's bond.

"Deborah," Aaron murmured one afternoon, his voice raspy but clear.

She nearly dropped her knitting in surprise. "Yes, Aaron?"

"Thank you," he said, his brown eyes locking onto hers. "For being here."

"Always," she promised, squeezing his hand with a tenderness that spoke volumes.

DEBORAH SAT BESIDE Aaron's bed, her knitting needles clicking softly as she worked on another pair of socks for the winter. She looked up when she felt a gentle squeeze on her hand.

"Deborah," Aaron whispered.

She set aside her knitting, her heart leaping. "Aaron?"

"Your hands..." He tried to sit up, his gaze focusing on the half-finished socks in her lap. "You've been busy."

"Rest now," she said, easing him back onto his pillow with a soft touch. "I had good company."

"Outsiders?" His brow knitted together, concern flickering across his features.

"Taken care of," she assured him. "You needn't worry."

A slow smile spread across his rugged face, and he reached out to stroke her cheek with a roughened fingertip. "Proud of you," he murmured.

"Thank you," Deborah replied, her voice barely above a whisper as a blush crept into her cheeks.

They lingered in the quiet comfort of the room, the only sounds the distant bustle of the hospital and the rustle of starched sheets as Aaron shifted. His fever had broken. The clarity in his eyes told her that the worst was over.

AARON LEANED ON DEBORAH as they made their way across the porch, his recovery still a work in progress. The other ranch hands were there to greet them, their grins wide and teasing.

"Look at this," Pete said. "The Gentle Giant laid low. Reckon we'll have to pick up the slack."

"Only until I'm back on my feet," Aaron shot back, a mock frown on his face. "Then you'll be eating my dust again."

"Sure, boss," Jim agreed, nudging Tom. "Let's leave him to rest. We've got a ranch to run."

"Go on then," Deborah said with a laugh. "We'll manage."

As the men ambled off toward the barn, Aaron turned to Deborah, his expression softening. "Seems like they missed me."

"Missed giving you a hard time, more like," she teased, helping him settle into a chair on the porch.

"Maybe so," he said, gazing out at the sprawling fields with a contented sigh. "But it's good to be home."

"Very good," she agreed, taking a seat next to him, her hand finding his once more. They watched in companionable silence as the sun dipped below the horizon, painting the sky with strokes of pink and orange.

"Tomorrow's another day," Aaron said, hope threading through his words.

"Another day," Deborah said, her heart full. "You have no idea what it means to me that we'll have another day together."

He smiled. "I'm home now. I'm just going to keep getting better."

AARON STRETCHED HIS arms, feeling strength surge back into his muscles. He watched Deborah through the kitchen window, her figure silhouetted against the morning light. Today, he would rejoin his men, and it filled him with a sense of purpose.

"Morning, Deb," Aaron called as he stepped into the warm kitchen. "Smells like heaven in here."

"Good morning," Deborah replied, her voice lacking its usual warmth. She kept her back to him, fussing over the stove. "Charlotte had to go help her daughter today, so it's just us."

"Something wrong?" Aaron asked, frowning at the tension in her shoulders.

"Nothing," she answered too quickly, offering him a weak smile that didn't reach her eyes. "Eat up. You'll need your strength."

He sat down, but his gaze lingered on her. As he ate the hearty breakfast she'd prepared, he noticed her untouched plate and the pallor of her skin. But before he could press further, she busied herself with cleaning up, skillfully evading his concern.

"Deborah," he started, but she cut him off.

"Go on, Aaron. The cattle won't drive themselves to Fort Worth."

"All right," he said reluctantly, sensing this wasn't the time to argue.

Outside, the air was thick with dust and the lowing of cattle. Aaron mounted his horse, the familiar creak of leather comforting. His men were already waiting, their faces set with determination.

"Ready, boss?" Pete asked, tipping his hat back.

"Let's do this," Aaron replied, the words rumbling from deep within his chest. He glanced back at the house once more, wishing Deborah stood there waving him off.

The drive was long and hot. It was already October, and it should be cooling off soon, but it didn't seem like soon enough to Aaron. They pushed the cattle along, the animals stirring up clouds of dust that clung to their clothes and skin. Despite the grueling work, there was camaraderie among the men—a shared joke here, a pat on the back there. They were a team, bound by sweat and the danger they'd shared.

"Hotter than a billy goat in a pepper patch," Jim remarked, wiping his brow with a dusty sleeve.

"Yep," Aaron agreed, squinting against the glare of the sun. "But we'll make good time if we keep at this pace."

"Deborah'll be proud, boss," Tom added with a grin.

Aaron nodded, his heart swelling with pride—and a twinge of worry for his wife left behind. But he shook it off, focusing on the task at hand.

"Come evening, we'll be in Fort Worth," he said. "Then it's just a matter of selling these beasts and heading home."

DEBORAH SAT ON THE porch, her hands folded neatly in her lap, her gaze following the path that led away from their homestead. The silence of Aaron's absence clung to the air like the summer heat, pressing down upon her with an unfamiliar weight. She turned as the screen door creaked and Cassandra stepped out, carrying two glasses of lemonade.

"Here," Cassandra said, offering one of the glasses. "You look like you could use this."

"Thank you." Deborah took a sip, the tartness making her pucker slightly. "I've been feeling off, Cassandra. Not just my stomach. It's like everything's topsy-turvy."

"Tell me about it," Cassandra urged, her voice steady and concerned.

"I can't keep much down, and I'm tired all the time. At first, I thought it was worry for Aaron, but now..." Deborah trailed off, her blue eyes clouded with uncertainty.

"Let's see Hortense. She'll have something for your stomach, at least." Cassandra's suggestion was practical, as always. Hortense was the local midwife who also did a great deal of healing with herbs.

"Suppose it couldn't hurt," Deborah murmured, allowing a faint smile to touch her lips as they set off down the road.

The walk to Hortense Blakely's place wasn't long, but the sun bore down unrelentingly. Hortense's herb garden welcomed them with its fragrant promise of relief. The older woman met them at the door, her keen eyes missing nothing.

"Come in, come in," Hortense beckoned, leading them to her cluttered kitchen where jars of dried herbs lined the shelves.

"Deborah's not well," Cassandra explained succinctly.

"Let's have a look at you, child," Hortense said, her fingers surprisingly gentle as she took Deborah's wrist, feeling for her pulse. "Let me examine you." She led Deborah from the room to her spare bedroom, which she used for checking the women who came to her.

After a short exam, Hortense nodded sagely. "Well, I'd say congratulations are in order, Deborah. You're expecting."

"Expecting?" Deborah echoed, the word foreign yet filling her with a sudden rush of joy.

"Indeed. A little one on the way."

Overwhelmed, Deborah felt the corners of her mouth twitch upwards. "A baby..." She'd noticed her cycle had been missing for a couple of months, but she'd thought it was the stress of Aaron almost dying.

"Let's get you some ginger tea for the mornings," Hortense suggested, already moving to gather the necessary ingredients.

By the time Aaron returned, the homestead seemed to hum with the secret Deborah harbored. She watched him stride toward her.

"Deborah," he greeted warmly, tipping his hat back with a familiar gesture.

"Welcome home, Aaron." Her heart beat fast as she stood before him, the news bubbling up inside her. "I have something to tell you."

He waited, anticipation etched into his rugged features.

"I'm... we're going to have a baby," she said, the words a bridge between them.

Aaron's reaction was immediate, his face breaking into a wide, ecstatic grin. He swept Deborah into his arms, spinning her around once before setting her down gently.

"That's the best news I've heard in ages!" His laughter rang through the air, infectious and full of life.

Deborah laughed too, her earlier reservations melting away in the warmth of his embrace. She rested her head against his chest, listening to the steady beat of his heart, and knew that whatever the future held, they would face it together.

Chapter Fourteen

Deborah sat by the fireplace, her hands moving with practiced ease as she knitted another row on the tiny blanket. The soft wool slid between her fingers, a pale blue that reminded her of the sky.

"Coming along nicely," she murmured, more to herself than anyone else.

She leaned back, resting a hand on her rounded belly, now impossible to ignore. It was Christmas, and the air was filled with a chill that contrasted sharply with the summer heat they were so accustomed to. Yet, despite her changing figure, Aaron's affection had not waned. If anything, it seemed to grow, much like the baby they eagerly awaited.

"Looks cozy," came Aaron's deep voice from the doorway. He stood there, framed by the wooden arch, dust from the ranch clinging to his boots and pants.

"Thought our little one might appreciate it," Deborah replied, her cheeks warming with a smile. She watched as Aaron removed his hat, revealing the tousled dark hair she found so endearing.

"Can't believe how quick you are with those needles," he said, crossing the room to sit beside her on the sofa, their spot at the end of each day.

"Only because I have good reason," she answered, her tone light as she folded the half-finished blanket and set it aside. For a moment, her fingers lingered on the yarn, the texture grounding her in the present.

"Everything all right?" Aaron asked, the concern in his voice gentle but evident.

"Fine as can be," she assured him, though she couldn't help the fleeting worry that crept into her thoughts. Would he still find her desirable, even as she expanded with their child?

"Good," he said, his large hand finding hers. "You're more beautiful than ever, Deb."

Her heart fluttered at his words, and she squeezed his hand in silent gratitude.

"Thank you," she whispered, feeling a swell of emotion for this man who had become her world. Together, they sat quietly, the crackling fire and the rhythmic ticking of the clock the only sounds in the room.

"Think you'll teach our little one to knit?" Aaron's question broke the silence, his voice tinged with amusement.

"Maybe," Deborah chuckled, imagining a future where their home was filled with the laughter of children and the warm embrace of family. "But only if they show an interest."

"Fair enough," he nodded.

DEBORAH LEANED AGAINST the wooden frame of the front door, her hands cradling the gentle curve of her belly. The ranch was quiet, too quiet for this time of evening. Aaron should have been home by now.

Finally, the familiar sound of hooves drumming against the hard-packed earth reached her ears. Her heart leaped, and she pushed off the doorframe, hurrying as fast as her condition would allow.

"Aaron," she called out.

"Hey there," he said, his voice carrying over to her as he dismounted. "Sorry I'm late."

Deborah reached him just as he finished tying off the reins. She searched his face, looking for signs of trouble, but found only the weariness of a long day's work.

"You had me worried," she admitted, her voice a mix of relief and reproach. "I can't stand the thought of something happening to you."

He wrapped his arms around her, pulling her close. "Nothing's going to happen, I promise. Just had to deal with a stubborn bull is all. You could say he was bull-headed."

She nodded, resting her head against his chest, comforted by the steady beat of his heart. "You're silly."

Later that night, after a simple supper of stew and fresh bread, they sat together at the small table. Deborah watched Aaron as he sipped his coffee, the lines of his face softened by the lamplight.

"Deb?" he asked, catching her gaze.

"Today, when you didn't come back on time..." she started, then paused, gathering her thoughts. "I realized just how much I need you. I love you so much, Aaron."

Aaron set down his cup, a smile tugging at the corners of his mouth. "Deb, I'm right here, and I'm not going anywhere." He reached across the table, his rough hand covering hers. "You and the little one mean everything to me."

Aaron's gaze lingered on Deborah, as though he were seeing her anew. The flicker of the oil lamp danced across her features, casting a golden hue on her swelling belly. Though she had voiced her fears earlier, there was something about the way she carried herself—a strength mingled with vulnerability—that drew him in.

"Deb," he said, his voice barely above a whisper, "I never figured someone could care for another person as much as I care for you. I love you. With everything inside me." His eyes sparkled with unspoken emotion, and in their depths, she saw the truth of his words reflected back at her.

Deborah reached out, her fingers brushing his calloused hand. "And I never imagined I'd find someone who'd fill my heart the way you do, Aaron."

They settled into a companionable silence, the world outside fading away. It was just the two of them, and the life they were building together. A soft smile played on Deborah's lips as she spoke again, her hands now folded over her belly. "Can you believe it? Soon we'll be holding our little one in our arms."

"Hard to believe," Aaron admitted, his usual stoic demeanor giving way to a gentle warmth. "I reckon this baby will have the best of us both."

"Maybe a bit of your stubbornness," she teased, a playful glint in her green eyes.

"And your sass, no doubt," he countered, the corner of his mouth lifting in a half-smile.

Epilogue

Nine years later

Deborah stepped onto the porch. She stretched her arms towards the sky, feeling the gentle pull of muscles that had relaxed during sleep. A soft sigh escaped her lips as she savored the quiet stillness that enveloped the world at dawn.

Around her, the ranch was coming to life. Roosters crowed in the distance, and the soft rustle of cattle could be heard from the nearby fields. Deborah's heart swelled with contentment as she watched the land awaken, the worries of yesteryears now distant memories.

"Another beautiful day," she murmured to herself.

Her fingers lightly traced the wooden railings of the porch, worn smooth by years of weather and touch. The scent of freshly churned earth mixed with the sweet aroma of wildflowers carried on the breeze, grounding her in the present.

"Ma, look! The calf is up!" called a youthful voice from behind.

Deborah turned to see her youngest son, Jordan, his face lit with the excitement of new discoveries each day brought. His eyes, so much like Aaron's, sparkled with the same honest joy that had first drawn Deborah to her husband.

"Is he now?" Deborah replied, her voice carrying the warmth of the morning sun. "Let's go see him after breakfast."

"Okay, Ma!" Jordan dashed off in a blur, his energy boundless.

With one last appreciative glance at the ranch, Deborah made her way back inside, ready to embrace the bustling activity that filled her home.

Deborah's hands moved with practiced ease as she whisked eggs in a large bowl, the clink of the fork against ceramic a familiar melody in the dawn-lit kitchen. Fluffy piles of pancakes already stacked high on a platter, she turned her attention to the sizzling bacon, its aroma mingling with the sweet scent of maple syrup that warmed on the stove.

"Ma, can I flip the next one?" Sally, her eight-year-old and eager apprentice, stood on tiptoes to peer over the griddle's edge.

"Of course, my little chef," Deborah said with an affectionate smile, stepping aside. She watched as Sally carefully slid the spatula under the golden-brown pancake and flipped it with a flourish. "Well done!"

"Maybe I'll be as good as you someday," Sally beamed, pride coloring her cheeks rosy.

"Darling, you'll be even better," Deborah assured her, tousling Sally's brown curls that so resembled her own.

As they worked side by side, the room filled with the hustle and bustle of breakfast preparations. Deborah poured milk into glasses, sliced fresh bread, and set the table. Charlotte was still with them, but she was helping her daughter with a new baby, so Deborah was in charge of the cooking for a while.

"Morning, everyone!" Aaron's deep voice boomed from the doorway, his presence filling the space like sunshine after a storm.

"Good morning, Aaron," Deborah greeted him, feeling a flutter in her chest that never quite faded, no matter the years. He kissed her cheek before taking his seat at the head of the table, where steaming plates awaited.

"Today, we're thinking of bringing you a picnic around noon," she mentioned casually as she handed him a cup of coffee, black as he liked it. "Thought it might be nice for us all to eat together."

"A picnic?" Aaron's eyes lit up, the corners crinkling with joy. "Now that's a plan." He took a sip of his coffee, savoring the taste. "We've got fences needing mending on the north pasture, but we'll make short work of it with a promise like that."

"Then it's settled." Deborah nodded, contentment nestled within her heart.

The children chattered excitedly, animated by the prospect of dining under the Texas sky. The simple pleasures of their life on the ranch were not lost on Deborah.

Deborah watched as Aaron readied himself for the day's work, his silhouette framed by the sprawling Texas landscape. The children scurried around them, their laughter mingling with the sounds of the waking farm.

"Remember to drink plenty of water," Deborah reminded him, concern knit into her brow as she handed him a canteen.

"Always do," Aaron replied, his voice a comforting rumble. He leaned down and kissed her gently, his lips warm against hers—a promise sealed in a simple gesture. "See y'all at noon."

"Bye, Papa!" Sally waved, clutching her little brother Jordan's hand while Sandra and Joseph chased each other nearby.

Deborah watched as Aaron strode away, his broad shoulders squared against the day ahead. She knew her place was here, within the walls of their home. Sally, at eight, mirrored her mother's nurturing spirit. Six-year-old Sandra inherited Deborah's contemplative eyes. Joseph, four, showed signs of his father's strength, and little Jordan, just two, was the joy that kept them all laughing.

Soon the family reunited on a blanket spread beneath an old oak tree. The children's giggles floated on the breeze as they played tag after finishing their picnic lunch.

"Look at them, Aaron," Deborah said, her voice soft with emotion. "This—this is what we dreamed about."

Aaron stretched out beside her, his gaze following the children. "It sure is," he agreed, his deep voice filled with contentment.

"Back then, it was just a hope, a wish whispered in the dark. And now..." her words trailed off as she took in the sight of their family.

"And now, it's our life." Aaron reached over, lacing his fingers with hers. "Our beautiful life."

Her blue eyes met his brown ones, and in that simple exchange, volumes were spoken. She squeezed his hand, her heart swelling with a love so profound it anchored her to this moment, to this man, to the land that bore witness to their shared dream finally realized.

"Couldn't be happier," Deborah murmured, leaning into his solid frame.

"Me neither," Aaron whispered back, and together they watched the future they'd built play before them in fits of laughter and shouts of delight.

9 798224 157334